A Bag of Lucky Rice

A BAG of LUCKY RICE

a novel by

George Reichart

pictures by

Mark Mitchell

David R. Godine, *Publisher*

BOSTON

First published in 2002 by
DAVID R. GODINE, *Publisher*
Post Office Box 450
Jaffrey, New Hampshire 03452
www.godine.com

LIBRARY OF CONGRESS CATALOGING-IN-PUBLICATION DATA
Reichart, George
A bag of lucky rice / by George Reichart;
pictures by Mark Mitchell.—1st. ed.
p. cm.
Summary: Rusty, an old prospector, and Lo Fat and Lee, two Chinese
living in the small mining town of Rhyolite, Nevada, become friends
and share the excitement of finding gold in the Amargosa Desert.
ISBN 1–56792–278–3 (alk. paper)
[1. Gold mines and mining—Fiction.
2. Chinese Americans—Fiction.
3. Nevada—History—19th Century—Fiction.]
I. Mitchell, Mark, 1951– ill.
II. Title.
PZ7.R26345 Bag 2001
[Fic]—dc21   2001055594

FIRST SOFTCOVER EDITION 2004
Printed in Canada

A Bag of Lucky Rice

CHAPTER ONE

New Friends

RUSTY DALTON was one of those old, hard luck prospectors folks often referred to as desert rats. The harshness of life in the desert made Rusty look older than most people his age. But he was a hardy soul who never complained.

One evening, Rusty wandered into Rhyolite, a small mining town in Nevada's Amargosa Desert. He walked down the alley behind the Southern Hotel, the best hotel in town. He went around back to the kitchen, where he found a Chinese boy sitting on the steps, peeling potatoes. Rusty smiled at the boy and knocked on the kitchen door. The hotel's chef, a short, plump Chinese man named Lo Fat, opened the door and said, "Lo Fat busy. No talk."

Rusty took off his hat, smiled, and said, "Got any work I can do for some food? Just food. No money."

It so happened that Lo Fat was having trouble locating help, other than his twelve-year-old son, Lee. The boy looked up at his father and spoke in Chinese. Lo Fat's eyes lit up, and he said to Rusty, "You — know how peel potato?"

Rusty nodded. Lo Fat disappeared for a moment, soon returning with a large pan and a huge sack of potatoes.

3

"Lee show you," Lo Fat said, handing Rusty a paring knife. "Food. No money. Okay?"

Lee showed Rusty a few tricks with the knife and how to keep turning the potato as he peeled it. Rusty got the knack of it in no time.

Speaking better English than his father, Lee explained to Rusty that the next three nights would be busy ones at the hotel. The governor of Nevada and some businessmen from the East were meeting to discuss some new and bigger plans for mining gold in Rhyolite. Lo Fat was busy preparing two big dinners and a banquet for the occasion.

Gold had been discovered in Rhyolite in 1904 at a place where rocks as big and green as bullfrogs dotted the hillside. Prospectors spotted small pieces of gold in these rocks, spread about as far apart as a bullfrog could jump. The discovery site became known as Bullfrog Mine. News of the discovery traveled fast, and Rhyolite quickly grew from a camp with 100 tents and 200 people in 1904, into a city with a population of 10,000 by 1908. Prospectors, miners, speculators, shopkeepers, innkeepers, bankers, and just about everyone else whom one would expect to find in a large town had moved to Rhyolite in hopes of striking it rich. In just three years, Rhyolite had banks, stores, and the best railroad station in Nevada. It also had a Wells Fargo Office and over forty saloons and gambling halls. The Southern Hotel became the town's headquarters and the central meeting place for new people seeking food, lodging, and information.

After that evening's big dinner party at the hotel, Lo Fat brought out plates of food for Rusty and Lee, who sat quietly eating their meals on the back steps. Rusty thought that the plate of food looked like rather skimpy payment for almost three hours of potato peeling. Lee didn't have much on his plate either, so Rusty decided it was wiser not to ask for more. As Rusty was leaving, Lee smiled and said, "Come tomorrow. Maybe sooner, okay?" Rusty smiled and nodded.

The next day Rusty walked into the Porter Brothers' General Store, the largest of its kind in Rhyolite. It had been established by the Porter brothers in 1905. After having left a store in Randsburg, California, the brothers had loaded an eighteen-mule outfit with merchandise for miners and then headed for Rhyolite. Three times on their trip, they had had to unload the wagons, carry boxes, packages, and heavy sacks across danger-ous spots, reload, and continue on their arduous journey over the Mojave Desert and across Death Valley to finally arrive in the boomtown out in the desert.

While Rusty was looking over the groceries and other min-ers' supplies in the store, Mr. Porter walked over and said, "Howdy. Anything I can do for you?"

Rusty wasted no time in introducing himself and describing with great enthusiasm the big gold strike he intended to make someday. Then he said, "Mr. Porter, I'd be glad to give you half-interest in my first claim if you'd let me have a couple of hun-dred dollars' worth of stuff, so's I can get started."

Mr. Porter scowled at Rusty. "Two or three times a month some one-blanket, jackass prospector comes in here and offers me a fifty percent interest on a claim he's gonna make. I found out a long time ago that fifty percent of nothing is still noth-ing. I'm sorry, but I can't help you."

Mr. Porter looked quite surprised when Rusty replied, "Well, Mr. Porter, I'll be back one of these days with enough gold to buy a half-interest in this here store!"

As Rusty left, Mr. Porter shook his head slowly and muttered to himself, "Well, that'll be the day. The old desert rat!"

Rusty remembered that a fellow by the name of Joe Wilson had a corral on the edge of town and that he had a few burros for sale. When Rusty arrived at Joe's place, he found him tying a small donkey to a stake well away from the corral. "Whaddya get for a good burro?" asked Rusty.

Nodding toward the corral, Joe replied, "Well, the way things are goin' around here, I'm gettin' $100, sometimes more."

"How much for that skinny little one you just tied up over there?"

Joe grunted. "Huh, that ornery little critter ain't even a burro. He's some kind of a durn little donkey. He won't ever get any bigger. I can't afford to feed him, so I just stake him outside where he can eat sagebrush and weeds." Joe took off his hat and held it out where Rusty could see the brim. "You see that chunk missin' from the brim? Well, one day he just up and took a bite outta my hat, chewed it up, and swallowed it!"

Rusty smiled as he looked at the little donkey and said, "What're ya gonna do with him?"

"Durned if I know," Joe replied. "He's no good. I sure wouldn't go out in that desert with the likes of him." He took off his hat and scratched his head. "I'll tell you what. If you want him, I'll make you a deal." Joe went on to explain that all the men coming to town wanted to stake claims, mine gold, and get rich. No one wanted to work for a few dollars a day, especially when eggs cost $1 each and water was $2 or $3 a barrel.

"Here's my deal," Joe said. "I'm fixin' to make my corral a lot bigger, and I've got a bunch of posts and rails down at the freight yard. Now, if you'll dig the post holes, take my wagon down to pick up the posts and rails, and put 'em in the holes, I'll give you $25 and that no-good donkey to boot."

Rusty reached out to shake Joe's hand. "It's a deal."

Rusty worked hard the rest of the day. Joe, who was busy shaping some horseshoes in the barn, checked on Rusty's progress now and then and was surprised by the determined effort and hard work put out by the old man. Generally, most folks regarded Rusty as a shiftless, no-account drifter, but Rusty didn't mind *what* people thought, and he always had a cheerful word for everyone. With half a smile on his face and a strange twinkle in his eyes, he gave people the funny feeling that he knew something that they didn't, and that he wasn't about to tell anyone what it was. So, while people laughed at him, they were never *quite* sure what to think.

Although Rusty's hair was turning gray, his shaggy beard was still a rusty color underneath all the dust. But the real reason people called him Rusty was that his miner's pick and shovel were always rusty from lack of use. Other prospectors had teased him because they knew that if he had been digging, his pick and shovel would have been worn smooth and shiny. Rusty's response was always the same. "Well, I don't see no sense in diggin' till I find somethin' to dig for." Then he'd turn right around and tell everyone that someday he was going to strike it rich and have more gold than any man in Nevada. The fellows mostly just laughed and called him a crazy old geezer.

Each evening after working for Joe at the corral, Rusty arrived at the back steps of the Southern Hotel, where Lee greeted him just like an old buddy. As they peeled potatoes together, Lee asked Rusty questions about his life as a prospector. The way Rusty described his life, it all sounded like fun. Finding gold and getting rich, what excitement! This kind of a life seemed strange and daring to Lee. Rusty might have looked like a tramp to most people, but Lee saw him as a brave and noble hero. Lee asked, "Gold in far-off place — no house, no bed for you?"

With a little pride in his voice, Rusty replied, "Nope, but when a feller gets used to roughin' it, campin' out just comes kinda natural-like."

Lee continued, "That hard work! Nobody pay you money?"

Rusty smiled and looked at his old, rough hands, "Well, these here hands will hold a sack of gold someday. Nobody 'round here's got that much money to pay me anyhow."

Lee's enthusiasm showed, and his eyes brightened as he predicted, "You be rich man someday, very soon, I betcha."

Rusty laughed, "I betcha? Where'd you pick up that talk?" Lee just smiled and shrugged his shoulders.

A strange feeling came over Rusty. For the first time in years, he had someone who listened to him and believed what he said. Just talking with Lee was tonic for his soul. Rusty turned to Lee and said, "You're the first person who believes in what I say. It's funny, but every time I tell the truth in this town, nobody believes anything I say, but if I lie, everybody believes every word I say." Rusty and Lee had a good laugh over that.

During the next four days, Rusty worked harder than he'd worked in a long time. By noon on the fifth day, he had finished the corral. When Joe came to look over the work, he said, "Well, you sure done a good job. I sold a mule the other day, so I've got the cash to pay you right here." Joe handed Rusty $25 and said, "Now, like I said, that little donkey is part of the deal."

With a broad grin on his face, Rusty said, "Well, he's so durn much better than nothin' that he's real good."

Joe looked at the donkey and then back to Rusty. "Ya know," he said slowly, "I just have to tell you that, considerin' all the horses, mules, and burros I've ever seen, he's the worst. If I was to grade 'em all from A to Z, he'd be a Z-minus."

"Z-minus, huh?" asked Rusty with an amused look on his face. "Maybe I'll just let that be his name."

Joe laughed. "There ain't no use givin' that ornery little cuss a name. I called him all kinds of names just tryin' to get him to move. I finally had to hit him real hard in the rear with a board to convince him to do it."

"I'll take him anyway," Rusty said. "And while I'm at it, could I get a little bag of oats for a dollar or so?"

"Oats?" Joe asked. "I don't know where you come from, but out here in this high country, the bunch grass and white sagebrush is real good for horses and cattle."

Rusty looked at Z-minus and said, "You're right about that, but Z-minus here looks like he's minus a little meat on his ribs, and I figgered . . ."

Joe interrupted. "Naw, just keep your money. You done a durn good job for it. I'll get you a small bag of oats, but you'd be better off eatin' 'em yourself!" Joe laughed at his own joke. "I've got his packsaddle here somewhere. It's too small for a burro, so it's yours, too."

Rusty patted Z-minus on the neck and looked him over like he'd just bought a brand new car. Joe handed Rusty the bag of oats and put the packsaddle on the donkey's back. While Joe was busy cinching it up, Rusty opened the bag and offered Z-minus some oats.

Rusty smiled. "Look at the little feller eat them oats!"

Stepping five or six feet away, Rusty held out another handful. Z-minus might have been ornery, but he certainly wasn't stupid. He stepped up and ate the oats right out of Rusty's hand. Joe just shook his head and watched. Rusty dropped the lead rope and walked over by the corral's open gate. Z-minus was there almost before Rusty could get his hand into the sack of oats.

Then Rusty slowly walked out of the gate and down the road. The oat bag swung at his side as he walked along without stopping or turning around. Z-minus waggled his ears back and forth, then trotted slowly behind Rusty. When he caught up, he bumped Rusty in the back with his nose. Rusty turned around with the biggest smile ever. As he put out a handful of oats, Rusty yelled, "Well, Joe, I ain't hit him in the rear with no board yet. Whaddya think of that?"

With a sour look on his face, Joe called back, "The way you're goin', you'll run outta oats before you get outta town with that little cuss." Nevertheless, Rusty had a good feeling.

CHAPTER TWO

Off to the Funeral Mountains

RUSTY WALKED UP Golden Street, Rhyolite's main road. All of his belongings, which he had always carried on his own back, were now on the packsaddle. Z-minus followed right along, keeping his eye on the bag of oats.

Rusty smiled and tipped his hat to several ladies as he tied his donkey to a post in front of Porter Brothers' General Store. He walked right in like he owned the place and said, "Well, Mr. Porter, I'm back. I ain't ready to buy a half-interest in your store yet, but I've got $25 for some stuff I can use right now."

Mr. Porter was both surprised and amused, and he found himself thinking that he could come to like this old desert rat. Rusty bought the things that Mr. Porter thought he needed the most: beef jerky, a small slab of bacon, a tin of coffee, candles, matches, and a few other odds and ends. Mr. Porter helped carry the things out front, while Rusty rearranged the load on the packsaddle.

After looking at Z-minus and thinking to himself that the donkey was so little that he even made a small load look big, Mr. Porter said, "I just got to tell you that I'm sure glad I don't have a fifty percent interest in that donkey of yours. You wouldn't catch me all alone out in the desert with that scrawny little critter."

Rusty was getting a little tired of everybody picking on Z-minus. "I'll tell you one thing. He can make it out there in that old desert with less food and water than any horse."

Mr. Porter looked more closely at Z-minus. He poked the animal in the ribs. "Well, you might be right, and then again, you might be wrong. Look, we carry feed in this store. I'll give you a sack of oats for this run-down little cuss. You can consider that my fifty percent interest in getting you back to town again — alive!" He laughed.

Rusty gratefully loaded the extra sack of oats and thanked Mr. Porter. It was early afternoon, and the desert heat was intensifying. Rusty decided to go around behind the Southern Hotel where he could fill his two big canteens with fresh water and then lie down to rest in the shade.

Without really thinking about it, Rusty began to talk to Z-minus as if he were a person who understood everything he said. "There's goin' to be a real full moon tonight, so we'll travel by night and rest by day. We'll show 'em how to do it around here," Rusty said proudly. Z-minus snorted in apparent agreement.

Behind the hotel, they found Lee sitting on the kitchen steps, busily chopping up carrots and celery.

"No potatoes?" Rusty asked.

Lee was glad to see Rusty and beamed. "Potato later."

Rusty told Lee that he and Z-minus planned to leave town after sundown and head west for the Funeral Mountains in search of gold.

Lee considered this very daring, and asked, "Funeral Mountains, far off place. Safe place?"

Rusty smiled to himself because he wasn't used to anyone

being concerned about his safety. He reassured Lee. "Well, they're a long string of mountains, and Death Valley's right on the other side of 'em. They ain't so far off. Maybe twenty miles west, as the crow flies."

Puzzled, Lee asked, "Why crow fly there?"

Rusty chuckled. "You just hit on somethin'. No crow in his right mind would fly for twenty miles to get to Death Valley. In summer it's one of the hottest and driest places in this whole world. The Indians call it 'Tomesha.'"

"Tomesha?"

"Yeah, that's their way of sayin' 'ground on fire.'"

Lee was fascinated by Rusty's stories of strange places and people. And to think that Rusty's little donkey was going on this great adventure, too!

Lee put down his big chopping board and knife and stood right next to Z-minus, comparing his height to that of the little donkey. From the look in Lee's eyes it was clear that he wished he had a donkey like Z-Minus. Just then the door opened, and Lo Fat stepped out. In Chinese, Lee quickly told his father all about Rusty's plans.

Lo Fat smiled at Rusty. "Peel potato now. Okay?"

"Well, I sure need another dinner under my belt 'fore I leave." Rusty tied Z-minus to a pipe in the back of the building and gave him a couple handfuls of oats. After another three-hour stint of peeling potatoes, Rusty and Lee ate their skimpy dinners together on the back steps. While Rusty filled his canteens with water, Lo Fat came out on the back steps and held out a four- or five-pound bag of rice for Rusty. He spoke to Lee in Chinese.

Lee turned to Rusty and said, "This rice, my fatha rice. Not hotel rice. He say, rice good. Keep long time for you. Okay?"

Rusty thanked Lo Fat and put out his hand to his generous friend. Lo Fat smiled broadly at Rusty's gesture. Then, to Rusty's surprise, Lo Fat held his own two hands together and moved them up and down slightly. Rusty bowed awkwardly and smiled back. When Lo Fat smiled back, his cheeks were so full and round that his eyes closed. Finally, Lo Fat said, "China people say, 'Give rice, give good luck!'" Then he turned and went back into the kitchen.

Rusty added the "good luck rice" to Z's load, patted Lee on the head, and started down the street. Z-minus followed close behind.

The sun was setting as Rusty and Z slowly made their way west out of town toward a long ridge of mountains. Rusty planned to do most of his traveling at night to avoid the daytime heat. He talked out loud to Z-minus because hearing the sound of his own voice made it seem like he wasn't all alone. "See that long ridge over there? We'll be crossing over it about 10 o'clock tonight. The full moon lights this old desert up just dandy for walkin'! We won't get so hot and thirsty this way — we can save our water. The wild critters loaf around all day in the shade and come out at night when it's cool, so we'd better keep our eyes peeled for snakes. Them durn rattlers like to lie around on the warm sand soon as the sun's down. Seems like it's only people that ain't got enough sense to stay outta the hot sun in the middle of the day."

Z-minus followed along behind Rusty without stopping or being ornery and stubborn like Joe said he'd be. At the top of the ridge, Rusty stopped and got out the oats that Joe had given him. He looked at his pocket watch and said, "Well, pardner, we made it to the top of this ridge just 'bout 10 o'clock on the nose. Now, a steady little feller like you oughtta have a rest and some of these oats you're so crazy 'bout."

Rusty looked back at the lights in Rhyolite's saloons and gambling places. He hated the idea that he might have to return empty-handed in two or three weeks. In the past this had not bothered him. He was used to people thinking of him as a ne'er-do-well and a failure. But somehow his new friends, Lee and Lo Fat, made a big difference. They had wished him good luck and had great confidence in him. Rusty had no living relatives and no real friends. As he looked back at Rhyolite, he could see the lights of the Southern Hotel, where, at last, he had two *real* friends.

It wasn't long before Z-minus had finished his oats and started to walk ahead. Rusty took a few fast steps to get out in front. "Who's more anxious to find this durn gold, you or me?" Z snorted and trotted on, leaving Rusty scrambling to keep up.

During the night they crossed the broad valley west of the ridge. About sunup, they came to an outcropping of some large rocks at the foot of the mountains. Rusty took the load and the packsaddle off his little friend's back. After a bite to eat, they rested in the shade of the big rocks, which was a lucky stop because there were no trees for miles around. Rusty slept while Z-minus stood in the shade munching bunch grass with his eyes half-shut.

For the next two nights, they traveled along the edge of the Amargosa Desert at the foot of the Funeral Mountains. Rusty knew that Death Valley lay to the west on the other side of the mountains. Few people traveled in Death Valley, and even fewer stopped to look around, as Rusty did.

On the morning of the fourth day, Rusty decided that they

had better move a little higher up the mountain where he could get a better view of things. The greenhorns who came through this part of the country always looked for springs and water in the lowest part of the valley. Rusty used to laugh at them. "Did you ever see a waterfall in the bottom of a valley? Well, springs are sorta like waterfalls, Z. You find 'em part way up a mountain." So, Rusty gradually worked his way up higher and higher. Last winter, these mountains had received a lot of snow, but not a drop of rain had fallen in the two deserts on either side of them.

Late in the afternoon, Rusty's eye caught something moving in the distance. Stopping in his tracks, he squinted as he carefully followed the movement. Grinning, he watched two deer walk with their heads up and then disappear into a small ravine.

Rusty patted Z-minus on the neck and said, "Well, little feller, if you don't get a nice cold drink of spring water inside an hour, my name ain't Rusty Dalton!"

Rusty knew that when deer are running they are usually "runnin' scared." If they stand around, nibble for a bit, put their heads up, and then put them down again to nibble, they are just "pokin' around." But, when they walk steadily, in single file, with their heads up, chances are they're "headin' for water."

Rusty and Z-minus crossed a spur of the mountain. It was slow going over loose rocks, but Z-minus surprised Rusty with his willingness to plug along. After about half an hour, they reached a point where they could look up the length of the ravine. Part way up, Rusty spotted what he'd been looking for all day — green — dark green vegetation! The small clump of willows meant they were near water!

By the time they reached the willows, the deer were gone, but there was a spring, all right. Only a thin trickle of water ran down the face of a rocky ledge. Rusty caught some water in his hand and splashed a little in Z's face. Alerted, Z-Minus stepped up quickly and started licking the dripping wet stones.

Judging from the dwarfed size of the willows, Rusty figured that the spring probably dried up each year. The present trickle was now more than he and Z needed, but he guessed it would be gone in another month or two. Rusty grabbed his pick and knocked some of the rocks away from the bottom of the ledge, making room for his bucket, into which the water dripped. In less than five minutes, Rusty had a full bucket of cold water.

After looking the place over, Rusty decided that this could be a good location for their camp. It had water, shade, and a mountainside of loose rocks, making it ideal for finding gold ore. The best shady spot in the small but deep ravine was only about fifty yards from the spring. It was a fairly level space at the foot of a boulder the size of a two-story house. Loose rocks could slide down the steep mountain on either side of the boulder but not over it, which was probably why the space was so level.

Rusty climbed up the side of the ravine and onto the top of the big boulder. From there, he could see for miles in all directions. Behind him, in the west, were two mountain peaks, both over 6,000 feet high. In the opposite direction, he could see a big, dry lake bed in the broad desert valley below. The three-and-a-half-mile-long lake bed was chalky white and flat as a pancake. The Funeral Mountains benefited from just enough snowfall each year to feed a few small springs. No rivers or lakes existed in these rocky, barren desert mountains. If there were a tree growing in the area, no one had found it yet.

As Rusty looked over the desert, the thought came to him that this was just the kind of hideout the old stagecoach robbers would have liked. It was hidden in a ravine, had water, shade, and a lookout spot atop the big rock from which you could see for miles. As he climbed down off the boulder, he chuckled to himself, "This is a real robber's roost if I ever seen one."

With cool water and a sack of oats nearby, Rusty figured that Z-minus would stick close to camp without being tied to anything. He removed the load, packsaddle, and even the bridle. Giving Z a few handfuls of oats, he said, "Well, little pardner, this is our camp, and we'll make out fine here so long as we stick together."

After he put the camp in order, Rusty decided to bed down with his one blanket and get some rest. As he looked up at the stars, he began to think about his new friends. Had he bragged too much about finding gold? Thinking over Lee's funny little remark, Rusty thought to himself, "Well, I'm sure gonna give it a good try, I betcha."

CHAPTER THREE

From Z-Minus to A-Plus

RUSTY AWOKE before sunup. On his way to the spring for water to make coffee, he noticed that Z-minus was gone. Forgetting all about the coffee, Rusty started yelling, "Z! Z-minus! Where are you? Z-minus, come back here! Z, you ornery little cuss, you hear me? Z! Z-minus!"

Just then, he heard a banging sound from the other side of the clump of willows. Sure enough, there he spotted two long ears waggling back and forth.

"You ornery little critter, whaddya doin' down there?" Rusty yelled.

The banging continued, so Rusty yanked off the old Indian moccasins he wore at night and pulled on his hobnail boots. He hurried over and found that Z-minus had caught his right rear hoof in between some rocks and a hard, metal object. Z-minus was trying to kick free, but his hoof would not come loose. Rusty stooped down on his hands and knees to look more closely at the situation. He removed several small rocks, finally dislodged a big rock, and, toppling it over, freed Z-minus.

"You see, the minute I turn you loose, you go and get in a peck of trouble!" Rusty scolded.

Rusty banged on the side of the metal object, but it would not budge. He could see that it was part of something larger. He went to find his pick and shovel, wondering what this metal thing might be and how it ended up way out here in the desert.

As he dug the dirt and rocks away from the rusty old piece of black iron, he could see that it was one end of a large chest. Could it be a strongbox? He loosened the top with his rock pick and slowly pried open the lid. At first, it looked like the box was full of sand covered by a layer of dust.

Rusty poked his finger in the sand to see if it might be covering something. The cool sand felt strange to him. He scooped some into his hand. It seemed heavy. He fell down on his knees to scoop more into both hands. He shifted the sand around and let it run through his fingers. A broad grin spread slowly across his face. "Goldurn it, Z-minus, if this stuff don't look like gold!"

Rusty ran to camp for his old frying pan and then to the spring to put a little water in it. By the time he trotted back to the big iron box, his hands were trembling so much that he could hardly hold the pan steady and put the sand into it. He shook the pan back and forth, just like he was panning for gold. Gold, being heavy, would settle to the bottom of the pan, while everything else would spill over the edge of the pan with the water. This stuff settled in the bottom of the pan and stayed there. Nothing spilled over the edge, and the water in the pan remained almost clear. Rusty exclaimed to Z-minus, "I been drinkin' dirtier water than this fer years! This ain't gold ore. It's pure gold!"

Rusty picked out a few pieces of gold the size of peas and some about the size of apple seeds. But most of it was finer — pure gold dust. Then he let out a shout loud enough to scare every jackrabbit for miles around. "Z-minus, you discovered gold — pure gold!"

He jumped up and down, did a funny little jig, then clasped his hands over his stomach as he roared with laughter. Z-minus, who usually looked half-asleep, opened his eyes wide, put his head up high, and let out a loud, "Hee-haw! Hee-haw!"

Rusty picked up a handful of gold dust and yelled, "Pure gold! Pure gold! We're rich! We're rich!"

He just couldn't control himself. He doubled up laughing again, and as he did his little jig, Z-minus sounded off again, "Hee-haw! Hee-haw!"

Finally, Rusty settled down and turned to Z-minus. "When we get back to town, I'm gonna buy you enough oats to feed a twenty-mule team."

Z-minus nuzzled Rusty's pocket. "You ornery little critter. I'm beginnin' to think you understand everything I say."

Rusty was so mixed up he hardly knew what to do next. He put his arm around his little partner's neck and said, "Instead of Z-minus, your name oughtta be A-plus. I'll be danged if I'll ever call you Z-minus again, long as I live."

Rusty sat down on a rock and looked at the gold in the chest. He realized that he and his little donkey could never carry the big iron box back to town, even if it was empty. It was much bigger and heavier than the Wells Fargo strongboxes that were carried on the old stagecoaches. It left Rusty wondering where such a box could have come from.

"Well, little pardner," he said, "I guess we'll have to make a few more trips than I'd planned." He continued slowly, "If we was to get all that gold back to town in one trip, everybody'd wonder where we got it. It ain't ore. It's gold that's been panned. Nobody could pan that much gold in the few days we been gone. Yep, it's gonna take haulin' just a few sacks at a time, or folks will get mighty suspicious."

Rusty put the donkey's bridle back on and said, "Now, I got a little job for you." He led his little partner down to the clump of willows and tied him to one of the large branches.

"You're gonna like this job," Rusty said. "In the next couple of days I want you to eat every leaf in this clump of willers." Rusty went right on talking and explained everything to his donkey, who just stood there and blinked his eyes. "Gettin' rid of all that green won't kill the willers, but it'll keep strangers from spottin' our camp from way off."

Rusty looked at the gold again, closed the heavy lid, and decided to keep busy while he tried to figure out what to do next. He unpacked the sack of good luck rice, and his eyes became a little teary as he imagined telling Lo Fat and Lee of his good luck. Rusty had never cooked rice before and hoped that it would be about the same as cooking dried beans. He made a small circle of rocks and built a fire using dead willow branches. He put a couple of handfuls of rice in his skillet and filled it with water. Rusty was amazed as he watched the rice swell and overflow the pan as it cooked.

Rusty ate and ate but still had leftover rice, so after the remaining rice had cooled, he offered some to Z. "Well, since we're celebratin' with good luck rice, you sure deserve a little nibble, too."

The rice disappeared like magic. "That's enough of that. Next thing I know you'll be wantin' me to cook your oats." Rusty opened the sack of oats and let the donkey put his head inside for a few choice mouthfuls. "Joe Wilson said oats would just spoil you, but you know somethin'? If I thought you liked oatmeal better than oats, durned if I wouldn't cook 'em for you!"

Still in a daze over his gold discovery, Rusty talked continuously about anything that came to mind. He realized that he called his donkey "little feller" or "little pardner" most of the time because he had never liked the name Z-minus. Rusty considered A-plus as a possible name but then decided that, if he changed from Z-minus to A-plus, the little donkey might never learn his name.

Rusty watched the donkey nibbling at something on the ground and said, "A-plus, do you hear me, A-plus?" The donkey continued to nibble. Then he said, "Z?" The little donkey looked up immediately. Rusty wondered if he recognized "Z" as his name or if it just meant, "Here come the oats." Perhaps anything that sounded like "Z" would work. Well, he'd just have to sleep on that one for a while.

Rusty took off his boots, slipped on his Indian moccasins, and rolled up in his old blanket. A flood of thoughts ran through his mind before he fell asleep that night. How did all that gold end up buried here? Did it all belong to some miner who never came back to get it? Was it from a stagecoach or train robbery? Maybe it was from a lot of different robberies. Suppose the owners or robbers showed up while he was still here? Did any or all of it belong to Wells Fargo? If he took it in for a cash exchange or credit, anyone could claim it and give Rusty peanuts for a reward.

Rusty didn't doze off until well after midnight.

CHAPTER FOUR

Silence Is Golden

AS YOU MIGHT EXPECT, Rusty was up the next morning before the sun. The first thing he did was put on his boots and check to see if the iron box was really there. Maybe he had been dreaming. As Rusty lifted the heavy lid and ran his fingers through the gold again, it was all he could do to keep from yelling. This was no dream. That gold in his hands was real.

By sunup, Rusty had downed a tin of coffee and was frying some bacon. While his donkey stood nearby munching on bunch grass, Rusty started telling him what he'd been thinking about. "You know, we got to outsmart a lot of folks when we get back to town. We gotta hush this up somehow, or in two weeks there'll be 100 tents out here and in a month, 2,000 people, just like what happened in Rhyolite. Yep, we gotta outsmart 'em, you and me."

Rusty finished his last piece of bacon and filled the tin with the rest of the coffee. "You know, I used to have an uncle back in West Virginny, and my pa always used to say, 'Nobody ever outsmarted your Uncle Zeke, no sirree!' Uncle Zeke would know what to do with this gold."

Rusty suddenly jumped to his feet and said, "That's it! That's it! That's what I'm gonna call you — Zeke. It sounds almost like Z, and you'll get the hang of it in no time." He paused to think a minute. "Uncle Zeke Dalton, nobody ever outsmarted him, and nobody's ever gonna outsmart you, either. I'll bet my bottom dollar on that!"

In preparation for the trip back to Rhyolite that afternoon, Rusty filled his two ore bags with gold dust. Then he put the rest of the lucky rice in his skillet so he could use the rice bag for more gold dust. He placed the skillet on the top of the gold in the iron box. It just fit in the hollow where he had removed the gold. He closed the lid, and with a little work he managed to cover the old box with earth and rocks. For good measure, he threw some dead sagebrush on top.

After he filled the two big canteens with water he said, "We'll just leave that old bucket here to catch water for the wild critters!" As Rusty straightened the old bucket so that it wouldn't tip over, he noticed a large footprint in the moist soil around the bucket. He bent down on one knee and examined it more closely. It was clearly the print of a large paw. Rusty knew that it was too big to be a bobcat's footprint; he decided that it must be a cougar's.

Rusty looked and looked but found no other prints. The rest of the area was so rocky and full of pebbles that prints wouldn't show. After thinking it over, Rusty decided to spread fine soil around the bucket so he would be able to check for footprints when he returned. Finally, he checked his fire to be sure all the coals were out.

The trip back seemed easy because Rusty knew how far they could go each night and how long their food and water would hold out. As they walked along, Rusty began thinking about the tough guys who always hung around the saloon across from the Wells Fargo Office. They were the ones who always teased him about his rusty pick and shovel and his empty ore bags. Bringing ore in a bag to be tested is one thing, but bringing pure gold is another! He knew they'd cause trouble, if given a chance.

After the last night of travel, Rusty and Zeke stopped for an early breakfast — jerky and coffee for Rusty and oats for Zeke. When they were ready to head out again, Rusty said to his donkey, "Now Zeke, we're gonna outsmart some fellers today. Jus' wait till you see how it's done."

Rusty and Zeke continued the trip back to Rhyolite by daylight. Tired and thirsty, they walked into town late that afternoon. Rusty tied Zeke to the hitching post in front of the Wells Fargo Office. The two bulging ore bags hung over Zeke's back in plain sight. Rusty licked his dry lips as he unstrapped the two big canteens, swung them over his shoulder and lazily sauntered up to the Wells Fargo Office and walked in.

Mr. Kimbel, the Wells Fargo agent, greeted Rusty and said, "Looks like you've got some ore out there in your bags, at long last."

As they were talking and looking out of the front window, two tough-looking guys from the saloon walked up to Zeke. One of them opened an ore bag and took out a handful of its contents. He handed the bag to the other man, and after a brief look, they dumped the whole bag over Zeke's hind end and had a good laugh.

Mr. Kimbel was shocked. "Look what they're doing to your ore!"

Rusty just chuckled. "It's nothing but pure sand! If you really wanna see somethin', just take a look at this." He opened one of the canteens and poured some of the pure gold onto Mr. Kimbel's desk.

Mr. Kimbel was speechless as he scooped up a small handful to examine it more closely. Finally, he said, "Well, I'll be damned. This stuff ain't ore! It's pure gold! Man, do you realize what you've got here?"

With that old twinkle in his eye, Rusty announced, "Well, that ain't all. This canteen is full, too, and so is this." Then he unbuttoned his shirt just above his belt and pulled out the rice bag and plunked it on the desk beside the canteens. "Well, Mr. Kimbel, all you got to do is weigh it and lock it up for me."

Mr. Kimbel shook his head in disbelief as he weighed the gold and recorded some figures. Then he picked up the rice bag and rolled it in his hand. "$12,000," he said slowly. "That's what you've got here . . . $12,000 worth of gold."

Wells Fargo had handled much greater quantities of gold for big mining companies but never in his life this much for a one-blanket, jackass prospector.

Rusty looked at Mr. Kimbel seriously and said, "You know, Mr. Kimbel, gold is funny stuff. It's more fun findin' it than havin' it! Now that I got it, I'm headin' for a peck of trouble. If news of this gets out, I'm gonna have fellers tailin' me all over the desert, and I ain't through just yet."

Mr. Kimbel glanced out the window and then back at Rusty. "It's our policy not to discuss our customers' accounts with outsiders. You can depend on us to keep this confidential," he replied quickly.

Rusty drew out $200 in cash against his gold account. The Wells Fargo agent offered to buy the gold and ship it to the mint, but Rusty told him to store it and that he would pay the storage charge.

When Rusty went outside to untie Zeke, a few of the tough guys were laughing and joking. One of them said, "So, you're gonna be the richest feller in Nevada! Whatcha gonna run, a sand and gravel outfit?" They all laughed again.

Rusty laughed, too, because he had outsmarted them. About four miles before he reached town, he had poured all the gold dust from the ore bags into the two empty canteens and then filled the bags with sand.

Rusty's next stop was the back steps of the Southern Hotel. He and Zeke walked along much faster than usual with the help of a bag of oats, which Rusty dangled under Zeke's nose. Rusty could hardly wait to tell Lo Fat and Lee of his great luck. As he and Zeke rounded the corner, they found Lee sitting on the back steps, busy as usual.

Lee looked up, grinned, and called to Lo Fat in Chinese. When Lo Fat came to the back door, the three of them smiled, laughed, shook their own hands Chinese-style, and shared a happy reunion.

Rusty opened the conversation by saying, "I sure do want to thank you for that bag of lucky rice you gave me. You just won't believe how lucky I've been."

Lee and Lo Fat smiled, anxious to hear about the good luck. Rusty knew that these were two people who would keep his secret. He did not tell them about the big iron box but did say that he had found a lot of gold. "No talk," they assured him.

Then Rusty changed the subject. "China people think rice is lucky. Is it lucky for everybody?"

Lee translated the question for his father. Lo Fat grinned and said, "Rice lucky for everybody! 'merican people have wedding. Throw rice, good luck! Okay!"

Rusty laughed and replied, "Well, I don't know if it's rice or the feller givin' the rice, but if I had any more luck than this, I couldn't stand it!" He patted Zeke on the neck and continued, "We've gotta get on down to Porter Brothers' General Store 'fore they close, but we'll be back. And this time I'm gonna buy dinner. Okay?"

Lo Fat and Lee smiled. It was easy to see that they were amazed and delighted by their friend's good luck.

As they approached the store, Rusty saw Mr. Porter standing on the boardwalk in front. He greeted Rusty and Zeke with a broad smile, "Well, I see those oats I gave you kept that little cuss going till you got back to town."

Rusty replied, "Yep, them oats worked so good that I want a couple more sacks, and I've got the cash right here."

Rusty gave Mr. Porter a list of things he needed, including a new pair of heavy socks, a sack of flour, a bucket, and some odds and ends. Then he came up with a surprise request. "I need a new gold minin' pan; my old one's just about shot. And, I could use four of them small leather bags the fellers use for gold dust, just in case I find any."

Mr. Porter couldn't help being a little nosey. He sat down on a stool behind the counter, took out his handkerchief and busied himself polishing the gold pan. "Looks like you already struck it rich. Got yourself a claim out there somewhere?" he asked casually.

Rusty replied, "Naw, I'm just scratchin' around, just gettin' enough to get by on. What's out there don't look like no mine, so I ain't filin' no claim."

Rusty bought the gold mining pan, so it would look like he was panning gold. Anyone could tell that the gold he was going to bring to town had already been panned by someone, somewhere. Anyhow, this new pan would be better for cooking rice than his old skillet.

Rusty picked up a sponge about as big as a good-sized cantaloupe. He squeezed it and said, "What is this durn thing?"

Mr. Porter replied, "That? Oh, that's a sponge."

"Sure is squishy, ain't it?" said Rusty as he squeezed it again.

"Yeah, the women use 'em. They dip it in a clean bucket of water and squeeze it over their kids' heads to get the soapy water off 'em after givin' 'em a bath," Mr. Porter explained.

"Is that so? Well, I'll take four of 'em. Maybe I can stuff 'em under Zeke's pack saddle so's it won't rub so hard on his back," said Rusty with a twinkle in his eye. Paying the bill and bidding Mr. Porter a hasty good-bye, Rusty gathered his purchases and left to get Zeke all packed. Watching Rusty closely, Mr. Porter scratched his head and thought, "There's more goin' on here than he's willing to talk about."

As Rusty and Zeke walked up Golden Street toward the hotel, they ran into Lee, who had just been in the Wells Fargo Office to deposit some of his earnings from gardening work.

Lo Fat greeted them when they arrived at the back steps of the hotel. Rusty smiled and said, "You know, that food in your kitchen smells real good all the way down the street! This time I'm gonna buy dinner for Lee and me."

Lo Fat looked a little disturbed and said, "Lee not eat inside. Jus' out here, only place."

Rusty nodded. "Well then, we'll eat right here on these back steps. Okay?"

Lo Fat came back shortly with two dishes filled with food. Rusty noticed that this was much more food than he and Lee were given for peeling potatoes. Lee ate with chopsticks, and

Rusty dug in with his fork. After a pleasant silence, Rusty finally said, "Lee, I think I'm beginnin' to understand China talk."

Lee looked surprised and didn't know what to say. Rusty continued, "I'll betcha I can prove it to you. When your pa comes to the door, don't say no China words. Okay?" Lee nodded.

Rusty called to Lo Fat. When he appeared in the doorway, Rusty asked, "Remember that first night I peeled all them potatoes for food and you was so busy? Lee said somethin' to you in your China talk, and then you said, 'Food, no money. Okay?' Remember?" Lo Fat nodded but was somewhat puzzled.

Rusty continued. "I know durn well just what Lee said to you! He said he knew you might run outta food for the big dinner at the hotel that night. So, Lee said — and I'll betcha on this — 'We need help. I'll split my dinner with him.'"

Lo Fat and Lee looked surprised. Lo Fat said, "You know China talk?"

Lee smiled and admitted that Rusty was right. Lo Fat was a little embarrassed. He picked up the two empty plates. "I get more. No half-half, okay?" He quickly disappeared into the kitchen.

Lee turned to Rusty and said, "Rusty know China talk. Lee know English talk. Hear two men talk. One — he say, 'Rusty take gold to Fargo Bank. Gold not in sack. Gold in big can.'" Lee paused and pointed to Rusty's two big canteens.

Rusty looked amazed. "Y' mean they figgered my gold was in them canteens?"

Lee nodded, "Yes, he say, 'No water in big can. Gold in big can.' Other man say, 'Next time, catch Rusty in desert place.'"

"Well, there's a lot of desert out there." Rusty stood up and paced back and forth. Then he sat down again on the steps. He lowered his voice almost to a whisper. "Did the feller say what place?"

Lee was a little confused, but he did his best to describe their plan. He pointed in a southwesterly direction as he continued. "Man say, 'Maybe ten mile.' Other man, tall man, say, 'Okay, at laundry place.'"

Rusty scratched his head. "Well, that sure beats me. Ten miles from here there ain't no water or no place to do laundry. There's nothin' out there but a big wash."

Lee's eyes lit up in excitement. "Wash place! That what they say, big *wash* place!"

Rusty laughed. "Lee, a wash is sort of a river without water. Wash don't mean laundry. But, I'm sure glad you told me about this."

Rusty continued. "Can you tell me what them fellers looked like?"

Lee thought a moment and said, "One man so," as he held his hand up as high as he could reach. "Other man like so," and he held his hand down much lower. Then he added, "They have whiskey all over face."

Puzzled, Rusty repeated, "Whiskey all over their faces, one tall and one short. Sure sounds like the two fellers hangin' around the saloon 'cross from Wells Fargo."

Lee replied quickly, "Oh, yes! That where I hear new talk as I walk by."

Rusty rubbed his beard with one hand as he digested this information. "Yep, could be them all right. They look like bums. They got no beards, but they only shave now and then."

Lee added, "Oh, yes. Many whiskeys on face."

As serious as all of this was, Rusty could not help but laugh. "Well, Lee, it don't matter what you call 'em, whiskeys or whiskers. For them fellers, you'd be right both ways."

Lee laughed again. This was his second English lesson in one day. Pleased that he had helped Rusty, Lee said, "Maybe I hear more."

"Well, keep your eyes and ears open." Before Rusty could say more, Lee placed his hand over his own mouth.

Rusty chuckled and stood up. "Yep, that's right. Keep your mouth shut. If them fellers ever get on to you, they'll skin you alive."

CHAPTER FIVE

Never Say Die

THREE DAYS LATER, Rusty and Zeke reached camp, right on schedule. Everything was just as they had left it. The first thing Rusty did was remove the load and packsaddle from Zeke's back and put some oats in the new bucket he'd bought. He rubbed his hands carefully over Zeke's back but didn't find any sore spots.

"Well, Zeke, you're not much good at smilin', but I got a hunch you might be a smilin' right now with your nose in that bucket where I can't see you."

Rusty tied Zeke's lead rope to the packsaddle. Then he took one of the sponges and walked down to the spring. Just as he was about to take a sponge bath, he stepped back in surprise. In the damp soil he had spread around the bucket at the foot of the spring were three large cat prints. He looked all around with a keen eye. Rusty knew that a cougar would probably not stay near the spring at this time of day. He also knew that even in this barren country, a big cat would be hard to spot if it were lying quietly on the ground, because its color blended well with the rocks in the canyon. After a quick bath, Rusty hustled back to camp.

He had only a small supply of firewood, mostly dead willow branches. As he was kindling a fire to cook some beans and smoked ham, he felt twinges of worry over Zeke's safety.

"Y' know, we gotta have some rules in this here camp. With that durn cat prowlin' 'round, I want you near me." When he had finished eating his dinner, Rusty put another stick on the fire. "I'll keep a little fire goin' all night so's that sneaky varmint will keep his distance."

Rusty tied the lead rope to the packsaddle and moved it close to his bedroll. "Now, I want you to stand with your head over here and your other end over there. You ain't 'zactly the sweetest smellin' thing I ever tried to sleep near to." He paused. "But, I will say, you're the best little stinker in the whole durn state of Nevada."

After a day's rest, Rusty thought about what they should do next. If the amount of gold he had taken into Rhyolite was worth $12,000, the big box must contain another $100,000 worth of pure gold!

"Zeke, we just gotta figure out some way to get all this gold to Wells Fargo without having a bunch of fellers tailin' us out here and robbin' us!"

Rusty filled the two ore bags and the four leather bags with gold and tied them good and tight. He bunched them together in a row and rolled them up in his old blanket. Then he tied both ends of the blanket roll with ropes and placed it on the front part of the pack load. He emptied the flour sack into his gold mining pan and filled the sack with gold. He filled the rice sack last and tucked it under his shirt. After filling the two canteens with spring water, he and Zeke were off for town again.

Everything went well. About ten miles from town, Rusty stopped and scratched his head and explained, "Well, Zeke, here's where we drink up the last of our water. I get the feelin' we gotta do a little outsmartin' again."

Rusty filled the empty canteens with sand, leaving just enough room so that, if anyone shook the canteens, the sand would shift back and forth inside, sounding like gold dust. Then he hid the canteens under the blanket roll and swung a sack of oats on top for good measure.

The banks along the big wash were steep, and only a few places offered possible crossings. Lee had said that the bad men would be waiting somewhere in the bottom of that wash. Out there on the desert floor, he and Zeke could be seen from miles away. Rusty had no choice but to cross at the same point he had before. He and the little donkey bravely picked their way down the side of the wash. Just before they reached the other side, Rusty heard the sound of hooves.

Things started to happen a little faster than Rusty had planned, but he was ready. Two men on horseback rode down the wash toward him. One was lean and lanky and looked like a wrangler. The other was short but looked as if he could be strong in a fight. Their faces were covered with scarves, but Lee's description of them was accurate. "Well, now, if it ain't the richest desert rat in Nevada again. How 'bout that, Casey?"

Rusty recognized that voice. They were the same men who had poured sand from the ore bags over Zeke's back. They had seen him carry his canteens in and out of the Wells Fargo Office.

Casey rode up close to Zeke and poked the nose of his rifle into the load on the packsaddle.

The lanky one spoke up again. "Now, I'll just bet that you can spare a little drink of water for a couple of thirsty fellers." He climbed off his horse and boldly walked up to Zeke to look over the load. Full of gold, the ore bags hung in plain sight. The sack of flour was tied on one side of the load, also in plain sight, but no canteens were to be seen anywhere.

He laughed. "I see you got bags of gold again, but where are them canteens?" He poked around a little and pulled both canteens out from under the blanket roll.

Rusty was quick to say, "There ain't no water in them canteens."

Both of the men laughed. The lanky one looked Rusty in the eye and said, "Yeah, last time you was in town we found out you didn't have no water in them canteens." Then he shook one canteen and could hear the sand shifting around inside. "Yep, this is it. Catch." He threw the canteen up to Casey who, still in his saddle, was fingering the barrel of his rifle. Then he swung the other canteen up and over his own saddle horn and removed several short lengths of rope.

Casey pointed his rifle at Rusty and said to his friend, "Hey, Steve, why don't I just make buzzard bait outta this ol' geezer."

The lanky one replied, "Naw, let's just tie him up here. That'll keep him busy till we make it outta town on the train."

Casey glared at Rusty. "Well, you heard what the man said. Jes' lie down there nice and easy like 'fore this trigger finger of mine slips."

Rusty knew that an argument would only make things worse, so he did what they told him. Steve tied Rusty's hands behind his back and his feet together at the ankles. He did it so fast and pulled the knots so tight they hurt. Rusty guessed that he was an experienced cowhand, who was used to bulldogging steers.

"Say, that's a pretty neat lookin' toad jabber you got there," said Steve. "We wouldn't want to see you cut yourself tryin' to get loose." He took Rusty's hunting knife from its sheath and cut Rusty's belt, pulling the sheath free. Then he returned the knife to its sheath and put it on his own belt.

Steve looked around. At the edge of the wash, he spotted a dead tree with the stub of a big branch sticking out of it. He jerked and tugged at Zeke's rope until he coaxed the reluctant animal over to the tree. Then he tied Zeke's rope to a branch that was about five feet off the ground.

As the robbers were about to leave, Rusty yelled to them, "You ain't gonna leave me here to die, are you?"

Casey pointed his rifle at Rusty and laughed. "Naw, we're just gonna leave you here. If you up and die, that's your own doin's." Still masked, the two men galloped off, a "hootin' and a hollerin'," as Rusty would say.

Rusty lay still until he couldn't hear them anymore. Then he rolled around on the ground and worked his way closer to Zeke. "Now, Zeke, I want ya to pay attention. You never seen me tied up and rollin' 'round on the ground like this, and you know I always put on them old moccasins 'stead of these boots when I lie down on the ground to sleep." Rusty realized that he was just talking to himself, but he couldn't give up on even the slimmest hope.

He wiggled his feet as best he could to get Zeke's attention. "Zeke, remember the time you was so hungry you bit a chunk right outta Joe Wilson's hat? Well, there ain't a blessed thing to eat in this dry ol' wash."

Rusty wiggled his boots again, and Zeke leaned down and nibbled on the toe of one boot. Rusty got excited. "That's it, little pardner! But, bite the durn rope, not my boots."

Still lying on the ground, Rusty raised his head a little higher to see what was going on. "Hey, you're comin' closer, but that's a leather lace in my boot you just bit to pieces." Rusty kept up his hopeful chatter, and after fifteen minutes or so, Zeke finally snatched one end of the rope in his mouth and gave it a tug.

Rusty became excited and upset all at the same time. "Now you're gettin' it, but you just pulled the knot even tighter 'round my ankles. Bite the durn rope in half."

Maybe Zeke liked the taste of the hemp rope, or maybe this wasn't the first time he had chewed someone free, but in three or four more nibbles, Rusty was on his feet and yelling, "Zeke Dalton, you ornery little cuss, you outsmarted 'em again!"

Rusty jumped up and down and did a little jig. He could hardly believe that his legs were free. "Well, little feller, like they say, 'One good turn deserves another,' so now I'm gonna untie you. Long as I can walk, we can make it to town, even with both hands tied behind me."

Rusty soon discovered that untying Zeke's rope wasn't all that easy because it was tied to a branch about five feet above the ground. With his hands tied behind him, Rusty tried hard to untie the lead rope from Zeke's halter, but he could only reach under Zeke's neck and wiggle his fingers. Zeke backed away; he didn't like being tickled under the chin. Finally, Rusty grabbed hold of the lead rope about two feet away from the halter, but he couldn't grip it well enough to pull the halter over Zeke's ears and off his head. After several attempts to break the rope or the branch it was tied to, Rusty tried to per-suade Zeke to nibble on the rope around his wrists. Zeke just licked Rusty's hands and nudged him in the back with his nose.

Rusty struggled up the side of the wash and looked across the desert toward Rhyolite — not a soul in sight. He knew that he could walk to town by himself, get his hands untied, and return for Zeke, but on his way back down into the wash, he began thinking, "When the robbers find out they got sand instead of gold, they'll be back, madder than hornets. If they run into me on my way to town, they might kill me, come for the gold, and leave Zeke to die. Them fellers got so little feelin's they might even shoot Zeke well as me."

The hot sun beat down on Rusty and Zeke, and they had no water. Rusty knew the hottest part of the day was yet to come. He looked at Zeke. "Well, little pardner, it don't matter 'bout them robbers comin' back. I ain't leavin' you here alone."

The dry, sandy wash provided absolutely no shade. In fact, it was even hotter than the rest of the desert! Rusty finally said, "I'll tell you what, I'll sit in the little shade you're makin' for awhile. Then I'll stand up and make some shade for you, even if it's only for your head."

As Rusty got down on his knees in the small patch of shade, he grabbed Zeke's lead rope in his mouth. But then he stood up and moved closer to Zeke's head. Maybe he could get Zeke to bite his own lead rope in half. Rusty chewed on it himself to give Zeke the idea. Zeke didn't understand Rusty's strange behavior. He stepped back and shook his head, which pulled the rope from Rusty's mouth. Rusty tried it again, but Zeke just shook his head again. "Yeah, I know, you're shakin' your head 'cause you think I'm plumb crazy with the heat," said Rusty.

The midday sun beat down on Rusty's head and face no matter which way he turned. He looked longingly at his hat, which lay on the ground out of his reach. The two hours that passed seemed more like two months.

While Rusty sat on the ground in the little bit of shade cast by Zeke's body, he began thinking, "If the robbers don't return by sundown, they probably won't return tonight. I could cross the desert to Rhyolite, get my hands untied, and return to save

Zeke by midnight. But what if the robbers return in the next hour or two? What would I do? Why not just give them the gold in Zeke's pack if they agree to let me and Zeke go free?" He knew that they would laugh at the idea of his giving them the gold because they planned to take it anyway. But, Rusty reasoned, if he told them it was a gift, not a robbery, and that he would not report it to the sheriff, they might listen. They would have the same gold and not have to face up to robbery or murder charges someday. Then again, the fellow with the rifle was so mean and trigger happy that he might shoot Zeke and him before he could make an offer.

Time passed slowly. Rusty realized that despite all his planning, a terrible tragedy could soon occur. He stood up and looked at Zeke. That old twinkle came back into his eyes, and he said, "Well, little feller, I heard an old sayin' once, and I'm gonna let you in on it now. 'Never say die.'"

Rusty couldn't pat Zeke on the neck with his hands tied, so he leaned over, rubbed his head on one of Zeke's big ears, and whispered, "Did you hear what I just said?"

CHAPTER SIX

Gold Is Where You Find It

ALL OF A SUDDEN, Rusty heard a faint noise. He listened intently and heard the soft sound of footsteps in the sand. His heart sank. The sounds grew louder and sounded like they were coming from around a sharp bend in the wash and growing closer. He was sure the outlaws had returned. Rusty stood in front of Zeke. He could run. But no, he was determined to stick by his little partner, no matter what.

A small figure ran around the bend in the wash and into the open. In a high-pitched voice the person started yelling, "Mistah Rusty! Mistah Rusty!" It was Lee! Lee broke into a full run down the middle of the wash, yelling, "Mistah Rusty! Mistah Rusty!"

Rusty was flabbergasted! He let out a wild yell. "Lee! Hey, Lee! *Holy Moses*! I can't believe this." Rusty ran to meet Lee. They were so excited that they bumped into each other. Lee stepped back, looked at Rusty, and then looked behind him to see why his arms were in such an odd position. Quickly, he loosened the knot and untied the rope around Rusty's wrists. Rusty gave Lee a big hug.

Lee took the small canteen that hung from his shoulder and handed it to Rusty. "Watah!"

Rusty took the canteen. "Well, I'll be durned! You got some left?"

Lee said, "Full! I save all for you, and this, too."

Lee untied a small cloth bag from his belt and handed it to Rusty. The bag contained three apples. Rusty took a big drink. Lee took a drink and then looked at Zeke. He handed an apple to Lee and said, "Zeke, can't drink outta no canteen, but he sure could handle one of them apples."

Lee held out the apple, and Zeke made applesauce out of it before Lee could blink an eye.

Rusty said, "For the life of me, I can't figger out how you knew we was in trouble and where to find us."

Lee smiled and said, "Maybe just lucky rice!"

Lee started to tell Rusty about his adventure. Late that morning he had gone down to Joe Wilson's corral to pick up a bag of horse manure for his garden. While he was there, Lee saw the tall man and his friend ride up to return their horses to Joe's corral. He noticed that they had both of Rusty's big canteens. They dismounted quickly and hurried off to the railroad station. Lee guessed that they had robbed Rusty and possibly hurt him. He ran back to the hotel and told his father that he was going out in the desert to look for Rusty in a big river where there was no water. His father was worried and insisted that Lee take water and the apples with him. Lo Fat said that he would send the sheriff to find Lee if he wasn't back by sundown.

When Lee finished his story, Rusty asked, "But how did you know where to find us?"

Lee replied, "I go to river with no water. High up place. Then walk down. This way not miss you."

As they left the wash and headed for town, Rusty walked in front where he could see the outlaws if they returned. Lee led Zeke. After a few miles, they stopped to eat an apple. When Lee finished, he held up his apple core and motioned to Rusty that he wanted to give it to Zeke.

Rusty said, "Go ahead. Zeke will be your friend for life. He could eat a whole barrel of them apple cores!"

On the long walk back to town, Lee and Rusty talked while Zeke chomped on their juicy apple cores. Rusty asked Lee about his garden. "I don't guess you raised them apples in your garden." He kicked the toe of his boot into the hard ground. "Whatever you're raisin', you must have to plant the seeds with a screwdriver. This ground's harder'n steel."

Lee told Rusty how he raised watermelons in a little patch near their house. To improve the poor soil, Lee had asked Joe Wilson if he could have a little horse manure for fertilizer. Joe was glad to get rid of the stuff. One time, when Lee arrived to pick another sack of manure, Joe's fourteen-year-old daughter, Jamie, was at the corral. She told Lee that the watermelon he had given her father a couple of weeks before was the sweetest, juiciest melon she had ever eaten.

Jamie wanted to see Lee's garden, so she offered to carry the big manure sack on her horse's back. When Lee said that he had never been on a horse before, she persuaded him to sit in the saddle while she led the horse up the street. Lee felt uneasy about being so high off the ground. Seeing that Lee was nervous, Jamie told him to lean forward and hang on to the horn tightly.

Rusty listened closely as Lee continued his story. "I think she very wrong. I tell Jamie, 'Horse do not have horn like cow?' She laugh. 'No, no. I mean the *saddle* horn, right in front of you.'"

Lee explained that after they had reached the garden and unloaded the manure, Lee showed Jamie how he raised such tasty watermelons. She asked a lot of questions, and he was proud to share his gardening secrets. Lee had broken off a chunk of a split melon and shared it with her. Then she mounted her horse, waved good-bye, and rode off at a fast trot.

Lee turned to Rusty and said, "Jamie call her horse Beans."

Rusty chuckled and asked Lee if he knew the story behind Beans' name. "Joe told me that he gave Jamie that little Indian pony on her last birthday. Jamie thought that the little brown spots scattered around the pony's white neck looked like brown beans, so she called him Beans."

Lee and Rusty both laughed about such a funny name. "He's a frisky little feller, but Jamie sure knows how to ride him. She's a reg'lar cowgirl!" said Rusty fondly.

They moved along steadily at a fast pace because Rusty wanted to get back to Rhyolite before sundown. Excited about having found Rusty and Zeke, Lee chattered continuously as they walked. Lee told Rusty how his grandfather came from China with many, many other Chinese coolies. He waved his hand in a wide motion to describe the great expanse of desert around them. "They make great railroad. Over mountain, over big desert, like here. Now train go *all* way 'cross 'merica."

Lee said that his grandfather could neither read nor write Chinese or English, but he was very proud of how he had helped to build such a great thing as the railroad.

Lee and his younger sister and both their parents had been

born in San Francisco. "When I was little, I think, Lee — China boy. My fatha say, 'NO! Lee — 'merican boy!'" Lee stopped walking and looked at Rusty. "Mistah Rusty, what you say?"

"Well, Lee, I'll say you sure are one *real* American boy if I ever seen one!"

Tired but happy, the threesome arrived in Rhyolite before sundown. The Southern Hotel was their first stop. When Lo Fat saw the bedraggled travellers, he smiled so big that his eyes closed. Dashing into the kitchen, he returned with two plates, each heaping with ham hocks, navy beans, and a slice of bread with apple butter. Rusty and Lee welcomed the food. With his nose in a bucket of oats, Zeke was happy, too.

While eating on the back steps, Rusty asked Lee not to tell anyone about the robbery and the rescue. Other tough guys might decide to try the same thing. Most important, Rusty feared for Lee's safety if the robbers were still in town. Lee put his hand over his mouth again, which made Rusty smile.

Rusty couldn't pry Zeke away from his oats, so he finally took them away from him. They went to Wells Fargo and arrived just as Mr. Kimbel was locking up for the night. He opened the door again and motioned for Rusty to come in.

Once inside the Wells Fargo office, Rusty dumped the two ore bags, the four leather bags, the flour sack, and the rice bag on top of the big table in the back of the room.

Mr. Kimbel gave a low whistle when he saw that each of the bags was full of gold. He weighed it all twice and figured out the value three times before he exclaimed, "Why, you've got almost $30,000 worth of gold here. When you add that to the first batch, your total's about $42,000. This is incredible!"

Mr. Kimbel looked out the window and then back at Rusty. In a low voice he said, "After you left town the other day, I had the assayer come over here just to look at your gold in the lock box. He says it's pure gold, all right. He never saw anything like it coming out of this desert before." Mr. Kimbel paused and looked Rusty straight in the eye. "He asked me where your claim is located because he couldn't find it in any mining district records."

Rusty smiled and, as that old twinkle came into his eyes, he said, "Well, Mr. Kimbel, there's an old sayin' — 'Gold is where you find it.' Two fellers tried to rob me today, and they'll tell you the same thing. Only they found sand instead of gold!" Rusty laughed and added, "So I'll just keep finding my gold where it is."

It was clear to Mr. Kimbel that he wasn't going to pry any information from Rusty. He looked toward the window and then back at Rusty. "Y' know, the way news gets around this town, I'm afraid you're going to have some more fellows trailing you before this is over."

Rusty gulped but said nothing. After helping Mr. Kimbel carry the gold to the big vault, Rusty thanked him and walked out the door of the Wells Fargo Office, possessively fingering the account book in his pocket.

CHAPTER SEVEN

Just Understandin' People

RUSTY STOPPED BY Porter Brothers' General Store the next morning to buy a few supplies. He beat Mr. Porter to the punch by saying, "Well, I'm back again to put a little more on the old barrelhead."

Mr. Porter hitched up his pants and said, "Well, we got lots of barrels 'round here, so make yourself at home."

Rusty bought two canteens, some oats, a belt and a fancy bedroll with canvas on the back. Then Rusty surprised Mr. Porter by saying, "It looks like maybe I oughtta get some kind of a gun. We got a pesky cougar hangin' 'round our camp."

Mr. Porter's interest picked up. "Cougar, you say? We've got some real good rifles here. The hunters swear by 'em."

Rusty hesitated. "Trouble is, if that big cat was 'bout to jump my donkey, I wouldn't have no time to run and get a rifle. You got any pistols?"

Mr. Porter looked surprised. "Nobody really wears side arms 'round here anymore, but let me see. I might have one 'round here somewhere."

He brought out a fancy leather holster with an ivory-handled pistol in it. "A Mexican feller put $50 cash down on it and said that he'd be back in a week or two to pay me the balance and pick it up. It's over a year ago since he left town and never came back. I'll let you have it for $50. Like I said, nobody's buying these things anymore."

Rusty looked it over and said, "Well, it's pretty fancy, but how does it shoot?"

"It's a good pistol," answered Mr. Porter, "and I still have the ammunition for it. The carved leather and silver trimmin' on the holster are almost worth more than the gun. Them Mexicans really know how to turn out leather goods."

Rusty said, "Well, I don't have to wear it 'round town. But out where we're headin', no one'll laugh at how I look." Rusty tried the holster on for size; it hung low on one side.

Mr. Porter laughed. "You sure do look like a real bandit. Here, let me punch another hole in the belt, so's you can wear it up a little tighter."

Rusty rolled up his new gun and holster in his new blanket roll. "This is the last thing I'm gonna add to your load," Rusty assured Zeke.

Rusty and Zeke headed down the alley to the back of the Southern Hotel for one of Lo Fat's good meals. They found Lee sitting on the back steps again, but this time he was reading a book instead of peeling potatoes.

Rusty tied Zeke to a post and said, "Howdy, Lee. Doin' some schoolwork?"

Lee answered with a weak smile. "I study book here. No school."

Rusty looked surprised. "Zeke and me just went by the schoolhouse today, and a lot of kids was runnin' around there."

In a sad voice, Lee explained, "I go. Teacher give me book. She say, 'Better you study homeside.' Miners say, 'No China boy at school.'"

Rusty shook his head and picked up Lee's book. "Well, that's a durn shame. You know, when I was a kid, I never actually quit school. I just sort of dropped in and out. But I quit droppin' in after the fourth grade. By then, us kids know'd everything the old schoolmaster know'd! By the time I found out that schoolin' was important, danged if it wasn't too late."

Just then, Lo Fat came to the back door with a big smile on his face. Rusty held up the schoolbook and said, "We was just talkin', and Lee tells me he's gettin' no schoolin' from the teacher and can't go to the schoolhouse."

Lo Fat replied proudly. "Lee teacher, good teacher. Lee teach Lo Fat book. Lo Fat learn. Lee learn. All same time."

Rusty put his hand on Lee's shoulder and said, "Too durn bad I never had a young'un like you."

For the first time in his life, Rusty realized how much he had missed by not having had a child like Lee. He had never seen a boy work so hard to help his father. Rusty had never known any Chinese people before, and seeing Lee teach his father the language and the ways of their new country made a big impression on him.

Lo Fat returned to his work in the kitchen. Lee seemed disturbed as he said, "Mr. Rusty, you say Lee 'merican boy — rememba?"

Rusty answered, "Well, you can't hardly be nothin' else. You was born in Frisco, and that does it."

Lee was not satisfied with this as he continued, "But why 'merica have two kinds boy?"

"What two kinds?" asked Rusty.

Lee explained, "One kind have school; have many friend. Other kind, no school, no friend. Sometime think, why to study? But book is only best friend, 'cept Mr. Rusty, so Lee study."

Rusty was beginning to understand Lee's feelings. He wanted to offer some kind of help, "Well, now, it ain't all that bad. You got another good friend in Jamie. Maybe she'd help you make some more friends down at the playground."

Unenthused, Lee replied, "I go playground. Boys say, 'Ha! Ha! Ha! Jamie jus' watermelon friend, tha's all!'"

Rusty felt his anger growing, "Well, they're wrong." But that still did not help Lee.

"How to be 'merican, Mr. Rusty? What Lee do wrong? What to do? Lee want to do." Lee put his head down between his arms so they couldn't see his face.

Rusty lightly touched Lee's shoulder. As he left he said, "We'll do sumthin' — you can bet your hat on that."

Just after class ended that afternoon, Rusty arrived at the schoolhouse to have a talk with the teacher. Miss Holbrook was erasing the big blackboard as he entered the room. As she turned around, Rusty removed his hat and said, "Ma'am, my name's Dalton, and I wondered if I could just have a word with you for a bit."

It was obvious that Miss Holbrook was a little annoyed by this shabbily dressed intruder. For all she knew, he might have been a tramp wanting money. She replied curtly, "I'm Miss Holbrook. Do you have a child attending this school?"

"Well, no ma'am, Miss Holbrook, but I sort of got one that ain't attendin' your school. That's why I come to see you."

"What is the child's name?" Miss Holbrook asked skeptically.

"His name is Lee, and his pa is the cook at the Southern Hotel."

Miss Holbrook's annoyance suddenly vanished. Guiltily, she

replied, "Oh, yes, the Chinese boy. I gave him a book to study at home. You see he just wouldn't fit in here. The other children's parents, mainly the miners, called that to my attention."

"Now, the good Lord knows I ain't one to tell you how to run this here school. But I can tell you 'bout that little boy, ma'am. He's a good American boy. Him, his ma and pa, and his little sister was all born in 'Frisco, U.S.A."

"Oh. Well, I just *assumed* that they were all from . . ." said Miss Holbrook slowly.

Rusty looked squarely at her. "An' I just assumed *any* American boy could go to *any* American school. Now, Miss Holbrook, you're a teacher, and I bet, down deep in your heart, you believe that yourself."

Miss Holbrook bit her lip and tried to regain her composure as she replied, "Well, yes. I do." She looked at the floor. "But you see, our school is overcrowded. I teach half of the children in the morning and the other half in the afternoon. I'm having enough trouble as it is." She glanced out the window and then back to Rusty. "It would disrupt this whole school if I started a big controversy with the parents over one Chinese student. I'm sorry, but my hands are tied."

Rusty laughed and gave her a friendly smile. "Ma'am, I know what you mean, but just having your *hands* tied don't 'mount to much, long as you ain't *tongue*-tied!"

Miss Holbrook was at a loss for words, so Rusty went on. "You know, I never met no China people till I run into Lo Fat and Lee. But soon I got to understandin' them, and they got to understandin' me. An' let me tell you, a feller couldn't find better friends than them two. Miss Holbrook, I've found out that people just understandin' people is all it takes."

Miss Holbrook smiled and interjected, "Mr. Dalton, I'll

have to admit that I'm beginning to understand you."

Rusty continued. "When it comes to understandin' people, I got a hunch your kids ain't gonna get that outta no schoolbooks. They ain't likely to get it at home neither. You see, most grown-up folks are kinda set in their ways. Just like they say, 'You can't teach an old dog new tricks.' But kids growin' up together get a lot outta goin' to school besides book learnin'. They get a real good chance to know each other and get some understanding.'"

Miss Holbrook nodded in agreement. She had to agree with this unusual man's down-to-earth logic.

"Miss Holbrook, did you know that Lee is teachin' his Pa to read that book you gave him? You see, they really want to understand us and our lingo. Lee wants to fit in, but he ain't even welcome to come to the playground after school's out!"

"I'm terribly sorry to hear that," responded Miss Holbrook, sadly.

Rusty couldn't be stopped. "And it ain't just Lee that's missin' out. Your school kids are missin' out, too, by not knowin' Lee." Rusty shifted his hat from one hand to the other. "Miss Holbrook, these kids need *you* to steer 'em in the right direction."

She smiled nervously and nodded her head. Rusty had certainly given her a lot to think about. "There's a lot of truth in what you say, Mr. Dalton."

Rusty thanked Miss Holbrook for her time. As he opened the door, he turned to her and said, "Ma'am, I just gotta tell you one more thing 'fore I go. If you really *believe* in somethin', facing up to it ain't half as tough as you think. Thank you, Miss Holbrook." Rusty put his hat back on and walked out the door.

CHAPTER EIGHT

History Repeats Itself

USTY AND ZEKE stayed in town for several days to enjoy a little rest. One morning Rusty was up before the first hint of light was visible in the eastern sky. All of the saloons in town were closed and completely dark. The only rooster in town was still dozing. Rhyolite was sound asleep, with the exception of Joe Wilson, who was up much earlier than usual and quite busy. He had moved his horses from the stable to the corral at the rear of his property. In the far end of the barn, away from the corral and nearest to the road, he had a small blacksmith shop. In this shop Joe had shaped many horseshoes on his heavy iron anvil.

Joe was leveling a solid spot on the ground right next to the big round stump that served as a base for the anvil. When he heard the sound of approaching footsteps, Joe, peering into the darkness, recognized the two familiar shapes and said, "Where you two fellers been all mornin'?"

Rusty and Zeke walked through the gate. Patting Zeke on the neck, Rusty smiled and answered, "Well, my little old 'larm clock here didn't sound off like he's s'posed to." Rusty handed

Joe a small package and continued, "But we got all the makin's for you, right here."

Joe opened it and looked at the contents. "Yep, a can of black powder and a good length of fuse. That oughtta do it."

Rusty and Joe proceeded to shove the heavy anvil along the top of the stump until it was near one edge. Then with a mighty heave, they toppled it over. It landed upside down on the ground next to the stump. They placed a big rock on the ground beside the anvil to keep it in place. In the center of its base, now facing upward, there was a hole about three inches deep and three inches square. Joe filled this hole with black powder while Rusty cut a length of fuse about a foot long. One end of the fuse was bent and pushed into the powder, and the rest of the fuse lay flat and led away from the anvil.

At that moment, Jamie and Lee arrived. Rusty had told Lee about his plans with Joe to experiment with an anvil blast for the upcoming Fourth of July celebration. And Lee had gone over to see if Jamie wanted to come and be part of the fun. They arrived just as Rusty and Joe, with Zeke safely tied to the corral, were lighting the fuse and running fast in the opposite direction. Seconds later, the morning stillness was ripped by a huge "boom" as the powder exploded inside the anvil.

As the smoke cleared away, Rusty said, "Now that oughtta be enough to put another crack in that old Liberty Bell."

Joe laughed as he added, "Yep, and I'll betcha half the folks in this town never heard an anvil blast before." He continued, "Years back in Tonopah and Goldfield, anvil blasts was about the only fireworks we had on the Fourth of July."

Rusty smiled and added, "Yeah, that and a few drinks, I'll bet!"

As strong as it was, the anvil blast had only knocked the heavy anvil onto its side. Jamie and Lee were inspecting the metal to see if it was hot or cracked, as Rusty continued, "You know, an anvil blast don't sound nothin' like a stick of dynamite goin' off. It sounds like a real big cannon." He rubbed the side of the big anvil as he continued, "Course a cannon and an anvil are both heavy iron, and that gives a certain kind of a ring to the sound."

Impressed, Lee looked up at Rusty and said, "You know firecracker, how firecracker sound, no?"

Rusty rubbed his beard with one hand as he made a slow and sad announcement. "Now talkin' 'bout firecrackers, that's a real shame. There won't be no firecrackers in Rhyolite this Fourth of July."

Looking surprised, Joe said, "But I heard that the Porter Brothers ordered enough fireworks for a town twice this size."

Rusty explained, "You been down to the freight yards lately? There's over a hundred railroad cars sittin' on the sidings down there. Mr. Porter's spent the last two days lookin' for his goods. It's a real whopper of a mess."

Jamie could hardly wait to interrupt, "Now is the time for Lee to tell you his secret." Lee seemed hesitant to say anything, so Jamie continued, "We'll both tell it. Lee's got a lot of firecrackers. His mother sent them to him over a month ago, didn't she, Lee?"

Lee nodded his head but did not look very happy, as he said, "I think trouble, maybe. What to do?"

Lee explained how he had written to his mother and asked her to send him some firecrackers. She had sent them from San Francisco several months ago, and they had arrived on the stage from Tonopah. Lee wanted to have some firecrackers so he could join in the fun with the other kids in Rhyolite. Now he was the only one who would actually have them. This bothered him. He knew if he tried to give them away, there wouldn't be enough for all the kids.

Rusty pondered the situation, and finally he offered an idea, "You know, the Fourth of July is for everybody. I'll betcha everybody in town heard our big blast, even if they wasn't listenin'." Rusty scratched the back of his head and continued, "Shootin' firecrackers off, one at a time, just might be kind of a problem. How many firecrackers you got?"

Lee's eyes lit up, and he said, "Four string — four big string and two Roman candle." Lee was enthusiastic as he continued, "I know! I know! Shoot all same time!"

Rusty was curious, "You mean throw 'em all in a big bonfire?"

"No, no," replied Lee, "Like China New Year, very special way!"

Lee explained that on special occasions the Chinese people would hang long strings of firecrackers from balconies or second floor windows. When the bottom of the string is lit, the intertwined fuses continue to light each other as the whole string explodes in rapid succession from the bottom to the top. Lee was elated as he concluded, "Sound like many soldier shoot. Sound like George Washington win, okay!"

Jamie was thrilled, "What a great idea! Let's see if Mr. Nelson will let you hang them out of the hotel window." Rusty and Joe agreed that this was a good idea.

Later that morning, Jamie and Lee went to see Mr. Nelson in his office at the Southern Hotel. Jamie explained that Lee had the only firecrackers in town. If he kept all of them for himself, he knew that the rest of the kids would be unhappy because he didn't have enough to share with everybody. At Mr. Nelson's request, Lee described his plan to hang four strings of fire-crackers from a second floor window of the hotel.

After being ignited, they would explode in a continuous manner. "This way — Fourth of July for everybody," said Lee enthusiastically.

Mr. Nelson thought for a moment and said, "Well now, we'll have to give this more thought." Then he continued slowly, "Most of the buildings in this town are wooden. The wood dries out fast in this climate and that creates a real fire hazard. Remember that fire in the south end of town last April? Well, after the volunteer firemen stretched two lengths of hose to get there, the water pressure broke the hose in two places. A bad wind came up, and it looked like the whole center of town might go." Jamie and Lee suspected that their plan was in trouble. Mr. Nelson pointed to a big photograph that hung on the wall behind his desk and continued, "You can see that this Southern Hotel is a completely wooden building." Mr. Nelson took a couple of steps and looked out of the office window. He had a glum look as he added, "The worst part of all this is that boardwalk in front of all these wooden buildings." He shook his head, "If a firecracker dropped through a crack in that walk — well." Mr. Nelson glanced at the Cook Bank Building across the street. A mysterious smile appeared on face as he sat at his desk. "Maybe I can figure something out. Come back in an hour."

Jamie went home to change her clothes because she would be marching in the Fourth of July parade later that day. Lee, peeling potatoes, was sitting on the back steps when Rusty and Zeke appeared. "Well, Lee, how'd you make out with your firecrackers?"

Lee answered Rusty without much enthusiasm. "Maybe, one hour, I know."

Rusty sat down on the steps, "What's holdin' things up?"

Lee had a puzzled look on his face as he continued, "Jamie say, Mr. Nelson have something stuck in sleeve . . . maybe one hour not stuck anymore." Lee continued, "Mr. Nelson, funny man. He say, 'no', but he smile, 'yes'!"

Rusty thought for a moment and then began to chuckle, "Did Jamie say that Mr. Nelson had something up his sleeve?"

Lee came right back, "Oh, yes, but he not hurt!" Rusty explained the meaning of this funny American saying, and they both had a good laugh.

Rusty picked up a book that was lying open on the steps next to Lee. As he glanced at the open page, he commented, "Did you get another schoolbook?"

"No. My mother send book with firecrackers, all same time," answered Lee. He pointed to the large illustration on the open page and said, "See George Washington in little boat!" It was a copy of the famous painting of Washington crossing the Delaware River. Lee had now forgotten all of his problems and continued, "This a very best story. I read ovah and ovah."

Rusty looked at the book closely and said, "I remember that same picture way back when I was in school, but I sort of forget how the story goes."

Lee stood up and said, "I get more potatoes. Mr. Rusty, you read story. Short time story. Okay?" Rusty smiled and read almost four pages.

When Lee returned, he found Rusty enthusiastic and amused. "That Washington was a real corker, all right! Why, that durn battle didn't last much longer than a string of firecrackers goin' off!" Rusty rubbed his beard as he was thinking, "You know, this gives me an idea." As Rusty untied Zeke, he said, "Keep your chin up, Lee, and I'll see you later." Already Lee was feeling a lot better.

About three o'clock that afternoon, over 400 members of the Miners Union marched the length of Golden Street. Miss Holbrook and all of the students in the school marched along in an orderly manner right behind them. Both marches ended at the intersection of Broadway and Golden Streets, directly in front of the Cook Bank Building, where a large crowd had gathered to watch the rock-drilling contest.

Four large rocks had been placed on one side of the street in front of the Cook Bank Building. In this contest, one man held a steel drill in place while another man hit the head of the drill with a sledge hammer. After each blow, the holder quickly turned the drill for the next blow. The team who drilled the deepest hole in ten minutes won the contest. The crowd had to stand back a safe distance because sparks flew in all directions. They held the contest in front of the Cook Bank Building because it was a concrete building with the town's only solid cement sidewalk, where sparks were not much of a fire hazard.

After the rock drilling contest, Mr. Overbury of the Board of Trade gave a short speech. He spoke from a small platform in the center of the street. It was decorated with red, white, and blue bunting and had a large flag flying from a pole.

When Mr. Overbury finished his speech, he introduced Mr. H. D. Porter, who removed his hat as he said, "It is with regret and an apology to all of you that I have to say this." He looked disturbed as he shifted his feet around and held his hat behind his back, "All the fireworks and firecrackers that I ordered for this occasion are lost somewhere in that mess down at the freight yards. I'm awful sorry, and I got nothin' more I can say."

Just as Mr. Porter stepped down from the speaker's platform, Rusty stepped up to the center. He quickly lit a Roman candle, which he then held high over his head. The crowd was startled by the loud boom-boom of those balls of fire flying out of the Roman candle into the sky. That bit of excitement ended too soon. The children gathered around the speaker's platform and were yelling to Rusty, "Do it again! Do it again!" They could see that Rusty had another Roman candle in his hand. People were smiling as Rusty said, "Well, I'm gonna do it again, all right, but first I wanna tell you somethin'."

The crowd gathered closer and listened carefully. Speaking loudly and clearly, Rusty said, "Most of you folks here must've seen that pitchur of George Washington crossin' the Delaware River — with all them big chunks of ice bobbin' around?" Rusty looked around and was encouraged to see a number of people nodding their heads. "You know them British claimed that our soldiers hid behind trees and rocks to do their shootin' and that Washington was chicken! Well, that really got him hot under the collar, so Washington and his fellers crossed that icy river to show 'em a trick or two." The people smiled and were amused as Rusty's version of history continued, "That old King George had sent a bunch of hired guns down to a little town called Trenton. Now those fellers was s'posed to be crack shots. But it was Christmas, and they got to drinkin' and carryin' on most of the night. 'Bout sunup the next mornin', Washington and his fellers lit into 'em!"

The children listened intently, anxious to hear what would happen next. Rusty continued, "Those dudes was still 'bout half drunk when they crawled outta bed and staggered all over the place in their long underwear, lookin' for their guns." Rusty had to pause because so many people were laughing. He proceeded to sum up the story "Why, I've seen fights last longer in some of the saloons 'round here!" Rusty spoke a little louder as he continued, "Since Washington and his fellers did the most shootin' — if you listen now, you'll hear just how that durn battle sounded and how quick it was over."

Rusty lit the second Roman candle and held it high over his head again. Just as the sound of the last fire ball was fading away, a terrific outburst of gunfire erupted. The crowd gasped in astonishment. Little children hid behind their mothers. Four men who had just stepped out of a saloon down the street panicked. One man ducked back into the saloon; two others fell to the ground; the fourth one held his hands up and yelled, "Don't shoot! Don't shoot!"

The crowd turned quickly in the direction of the Cook Bank Building. After a sigh of relief, the people began to smile and laugh as they saw that it was firecrackers exploding, instead of gunfire. Mr. Porter couldn't believe his ears.

Four strings of firecrackers exploded simultaneously. It sounded like a real battle was taking place, and the townspeople felt like they were right in the middle of it. Bits of red firecracker paper were flying.

The smell of powder smoke was drifting toward the crowd. The older children rushed closer to this wild, loud display.

The four strings of firecrackers, each about five feet long, were hanging from the bank's second floor window hanging on four separate cords tied to a long pole. Jamie and Lee had lowered the firecrackers out of the window while Rusty was talking. They had run downstairs quickly, and Lee had lit two *punks* and given one to Jamie. A Chinese punk is a stick about the size of a pencil covered with dry fuzzy material that burns slowly without becoming a flame.

With these punks, Jamie and Lee lit all the firecracker strings at the bottom, so that the explosions climbed up to the top of each string. When Rusty fired the second Roman candle, that was the signal for Jamie and Lee to light up. They immediately scampered away and became part of the crowd. Pleased and excited, the crowd of people couldn't figure out how this whole fireworks display had gotten started.

When the "firecracker battle" ended, a cheer went up. The kids yelled, "More, more!" People clapped, sensing they had just witnessed a memorable performance. Rusty waved his hat toward the Bank where Mr. Nelson, holding the pole from which the firecracker strings were hanging, leaned out of the window and waved. He still had that funny smile on his face.

Jamie and Lee were jumping up and down, so that Rusty could see them in the crowd. Rusty waved his hat and smiled. Joe Wilson, who had been standing nearby, put his hand on Rusty's shoulder as he said, "Durned if you and Lee didn't give the folks some kinda Fourth of July after all!"

Rusty, who wasn't used to flattery, grinned sheepishly and replied, "Well — most of it was Lee's doin's. That kid's a real U. S. A. crackerjack, if I ever seen one."

CHAPTER NINE

The Phantom Gold Mine

RUSTY AND ZEKE began another trip to the gold camp that night. They left a little early for the first leg of their journey. They planned to cross over the ridge west of town by sunset. Rusty timed their trip so that they would reach the group of large rocks on the other side of the broad valley before sunrise. From there, he could see if anyone had followed them into the valley.

Back in Rhyolite, a bunch of fellows stood out in front of the saloon to watch Rusty and Zeke disappear over the ridge at sunset. "He's headin' out the same old way, and if he walks all night we can catch up on horseback by mornin'," said Big Jim, one of the fellows in the group.

Jim's friend Ernie replied, "That'll be easy, but we got to stay behind him and outta sight till he reaches his camp, or he'll just run us 'round in the desert till we give up."

The two horsemen started out bright and early the next morning. At over six feet tall and 200 pounds, Big Jim was a big man, who played tough and took pleasure in bullying anyone smaller or weaker. He only shaved once or twice a month and always appeared scruffy. Big Jim's belly hung over his belt buckle, and he wore his pants so low that it looked like they might slide down over his rear at any time.

His partner, Ernie, was tall but looked weak and underfed. While not exactly stupid, he was slow at figuring things out and didn't usually have a lot to say. As long as he hung out with Big Jim, no one picked on him — except Big Jim. This was the part of their friendship that made it last.

As they started across the ridge, Big Jim and Ernie had no problem following Rusty and Zeke's trail. Zeke's hooves made deep prints in the ground, and Rusty's old hobnail mining boots left distinctive tracks that were easy to recognize.

Meanwhile, Rusty and Zeke had reached the other side of the wide valley. From the top of a big rock, Rusty could see the dust Big Jim and Ernie stirred up as they rode across the ridge. Rusty squinted against the early morning sun as he watched the men carefully following the tracks he and Zeke had made.

Jim and Ernie rode for an hour or so, then stopped when they were almost in the middle of the valley. The riders dismounted and walked around in circles, looking as if they were lost. Then they mounted their horses and slowly rode around in bigger circles. They dismounted and even got down on the ground in two or three places. One, trying to find some footprints, even crawled around on his hands and knees. Finally, they rode back to the last place they had seen footprints, and after riding around in one more small circle, they slowly headed back to town.

Rusty chuckled as he climbed down between the big rocks to where Zeke was standing in the shade. "Well, Zeke Dalton, you ornery cuss, we outsmarted 'em again." Rusty's ingenious plan had worked, but he swore to keep it a secret until all the gold was safe in the Wells Fargo vault.

❖❖ ❖❖ ❖❖

When the two riders got back to town, they headed straight for the saloon. Everyone stopped talking when they entered. "Well, boys, did you find out where he's getting the gold?" asked the bartender.

Big Jim took a gulp from his glass and looked at the bartender. Everyone in the room became silent, and all eyes turned to him. "You won't believe what we're gonna tell you! Tracking that donkey's hoofprints was easy. But 'bout the time we got halfway across that valley, all at once they disappeared. We walked and rode around for more than a mile in all directions and not one footprint nowhere. Even the old guy's footprints was gone! They just plum *vanished*."

The boys in the saloon broke into laughter and someone said, "Maybe it got so darn hot out in that desert that they 'vaporated!"

Someone else laughed, "Ol' Rusty thinks a lot of that little donkey. Maybe he just picked him up and *carried* him for the rest of the trip." Now they all roared with laughter.

Ernie said, "You fellers can laugh if you want, but I'm tellin' you, it gave us a funny feelin'. It was just like we was chasin' ghosts and lookin' for a phantom gold mine."

Big Jim declared, "We're gonna talk to the sheriff 'bout this 'cause there's something mighty funny goin' on around here. All that gold and him disappearin' into nowhere to get it!"

❖❖ ❖❖ ❖❖

Rusty and Zeke made their way back to camp with no more trouble. They rested there for several days, so Zeke had time to finish eating all of the willow leaves near the spring. Rusty found some deer hoofprints in the moist ground around the old bucket at the spring, but no trace of the big cat's paws were to be seen anywhere.

After uncovering the big iron box again, Rusty set to thinking about their next move. Each trip back to Rhyolite was increasingly difficult because, by now, almost everyone in town had heard the news of his big gold strike. Rusty and Zeke had arrived in Rhyolite at about noon on their first two trips. After thinking it over, Rusty decided to time the third trip so that they would arrive about 4 o'clock in the morning. Not many people would be up and around that early.

He filled two small ore bags, four small leather bags, the flour sack, and a small oat sack with gold. Rusty figured that he had packed about 100 pounds of gold so far. He knew that mules could easily carry 200 pounds and a regular burro about 150 pounds. But since he didn't want to overload little Zeke, Rusty usually carried the four little leather bags, which held about five pounds each. So with Zeke carrying about 100 pounds, they began their third trip.

After two nights they reached the group of big rocks on the west side of the large valley, the place where they had spent a day resting in the shade after the first two trips. From here it was another day-and-a-half into Rhyolite.

Rusty figured that if they left this shady hideout at about 11 o'clock in the morning, they should be in Rhyolite before sunrise the next day. Anyone who might be planning a robbery would probably misjudge their approach to Rhyolite by at least eight to ten hours.

While Rusty rested in the shade of the big rocks, a great idea came to him. Why not move a lot of gold from the iron box in their camp and hide it somewhere behind the rocks at this location. That way, he and Zeke could make a one-night trip to pick up the gold and return to Rhyolite the next day. All of the tough characters hanging around the saloons knew about how many days each of his trips from town and back would take. Nobody would be prepared to cause any trouble with this new plan.

Rusty and Zeke arrived in Rhyolite about 3:30 the next morning. Since the Wells Fargo Office would not be open, Rusty decided to wait on the back steps of the Southern Hotel. Just as he finished tying Zeke to a post, Lee came running around the corner. In a hushed voice, Lee said, "Bad men. Rob Fargo."

Shaken by this news, Rusty asked, "When did that happen?"

Lee replied hurriedly. "No. Not yet. Pretty soon!" Lee motioned for Rusty to come quickly to the back door of the Wells Fargo Office. Rusty put on his holster and gun. As they ran, Lee told Rusty how three men had come to his garden about two hours ago. They had made so much noise that they had awakened Lee. From his bedroom window, Lee had seen the men take a big watermelon and break it into pieces. They had stood around eating the melon and talking.

Lee overheard their plans to steal three of Joe Wilson's horses, tie them to a post behind the Wells Fargo Office, and then break in with tools and explosives. Lee had run down to Joe Wilson's corral. When he hadn't found Joe, he had taken some ropes and gone to the rear of the Wells Fargo Office. He had found three horses tied up outside, but the robbers were not in sight.

Slowing his pace, Lee said, "I think to take horses, but no. Maybe people say, 'Lee steal horses.' So, I make hobby horses."

Confused, Rusty asked, "Hobby horses?"

"Oh, yes. Hobby horses not walk. Not run."

More confused than ever, Rusty replied, "Well, hobby horses sure don't walk or run 'cause they ain't real horses."

Lee said, "I see Joe Wilson make hobby horses, many time. Real horses."

Rusty was still mystified. "That beats me! How does Joe make hobby horses out of real horses?"

Lee explained confidently, "Easy to do. Take one piece rope. Tie one end rope on horse front leg. Tie other end rope on other front leg. Hobby horse. Not move."

Rusty laughed. "You've hobbled the robbers' horses. That's what you've done! But Lee, how do you know them are Joe's horses, instead of the robbers' horses?"

"Oh, little Beans are there. With otha two!"

When Lee and Rusty arrived at Wells Fargo, three horses were standing there. Sure enough, they were hobbled, and one of them was, indeed, Beans. At the saloon around the corner, the robbers were having one more drink for good luck. They were also checking things out to see if anyone was still up and around at 4 o'clock in the morning.

Rusty was sure that the robbers would return at any time. He sent Lee to Joe Wilson's house; then, in an old shed across the narrow street, Rusty hid in the darkness of its doorway. Just then, the robbers came around the corner. The faint moonlight enabled Rusty to see them plainly against the white building across the street. When they reached the back entrance of the Wells Fargo Office, one of the men broke a window with the butt of his rifle.

Rusty knew that three tough outlaws with rifles would be more than one man could handle and that he had to act fast. Since they could not see him, he decided to try a big bluff.

In a strong husky voice, Rusty called out, "Jus' stand where you are and drop them guns. The jig is up!"

"Says who?" asked one of the robbers gruffly.

Rusty quickly snapped back, "Ever hear of Zeke Dalton?"

Another robber cried, "It's the Daltons. Let's get outta here!"

His two partners agreed as they jumped on their horses for a quick getaway.

Rusty's voice boomed out again. "You fellers ain't goin' nowhere. Your horses are hobbled." He fired a shot into the air.

One of the horses reared up on its hind legs, pawed the air with its front legs, and came down with a jolt. The rider yelled, "Danged if he ain't right. Somebody's hobbled our horses!"

"Throw them guns down on the ground," demanded Rusty boldly.

The robbers peered across the narrow street into the jet black shadows but could not see Rusty, who was feeling more confident. "Now listen carefully. The feller that throws his gun down last is the feller I'm gonna shoot first."

All three guns dropped to the ground before Rusty could bat an eye. "Well, whaddya you know! It was a tie!"

Rusty realized that the whole situation had suddenly changed. Robbers without guns, sitting on top of horses that can't move, are trapped! He had to stall for time but keep things moving fast enough that the outlaws wouldn't have a chance to plan anything or climb off their horses. Nervously, Rusty continued in a tough voice, "Now, don't like to see no poor widow woman bringin' flowers to some feller who can't smell no more. So, any of you fellers hitched?"

Without hesitation, all three robbers answered, "Oh, sure, I'm married. We're all married. Even got kids!"

Rusty responded quickly and firmly. "Now, I want each of you to talk up and talk up loud and fast. *What's your wife's name?"*

One robber yelled, "Mary."

Another yelled, "Dorothy."

The third outlaw said, "Well, my wife's name is, uh, uh — "

Rusty interrupted loudly, "You ain't got no wife! Well, that narrows it down good."

The outlaw with no wife pleaded, "You got nothin' on us. We ain't robbed no Wells Fargo. We just broke a window by accident."

The other outlaws joined in, "Yeah, he's right. We ain't robbed no Wells Fargo or nothin'."

"You got me to thank for not robbin' the Wells Fargo. But the folks in this town don't take kindly to no horse thieves," declared Rusty.

Knowing it was time for more action, Rusty stepped out of the doorway and said, "You there, who can't remember his wife's name, hold your hat up good and high, and I mean high."

As soon as the outlaw held his hat up high, Rusty fired two shots, both of which went right through the center of the hat. Rusty casually blew the smoke from his pistol barrel. "Now ain't you lucky your head wasn't in it."

Rusty knew that, if any one of the robbers slipped off his horse, he would have to shoot him. Otherwise, this whole situation could turn around and find Rusty pinned down, instead of the robbers. He hoped that his gun shots had awakened someone who could help him.

It so happened that Sheriff Tucker slept in the back room of his saloon on Friday nights because there was always a fight or two. Since his saloon was right across the street from the entrance to the Wells Fargo Office, he woke up and started pulling on his pants at the sound of Rusty's first gunshots. Just as the sheriff rounded the corner, Joe Wilson and Lee came running up the street from the opposite direction.

The sheriff held his rifle, ready to shoot, as he yelled, "What's goin' on here?"

Rusty stepped out of the shadows into the moonlit street and said, "Sheriff, I did all the shootin' just so's I'd attract some help."

The sheriff looked at the three men sitting on the horses and asked, "What are you fellers up to?"

Answering for them, Rusty replied, "They're bank robbers and horse thieves. And like you lawmen would say, 'They're right here sittin' on the evidence.'"

Joe Wilson stepped forward, held his rifle in a ready position and said, "He's right, sheriff. These are my horses, and I ain't never seen these three men before."

Rusty and Joe stood guard while the sheriff handcuffed the men one at a time after they had dismounted. Then Joe and the sheriff walked the three robbers to the jail. After Lee unhobbled the horses, he and Rusty led them back to Joe's corral.

Awakened by Rusty's gunshots, Jamie came running to meet them before they reached the corral. Overjoyed to see everyone safe, she hugged Beans around the neck. After the horses were returned to the corral, Lee and Rusty said good-bye and hurried back to the Southern Hotel.

As they rounded the corner of the hotel and approached the back entrance, Rusty stopped abruptly and exclaimed, "Zeke's gone!" Having arrived at the back steps, Rusty ran his hand over the hitching post. "I'm sure I left him tied right here to this post." The light was on in the hotel kitchen, and Lee went in to look for his father.

Rusty shook his head as he thought how this wild scramble

for gold was making everybody crazy. Good, ordinary folks were now scheming, cheating, stealing, and shooting at each other for some useless stuff that came out of the ground. He wondered if gold carried some kind of curse. Rusty realized that he was more worried about losing Zeke than about the gold in his packsaddle. Just then, Lo Fat came out of the kitchen doorway with his usual smile. Rusty wondered what he could be smiling about so early in the morning.

"Oh! Happy! Rusty come! Happy, happy!" greeted Lo Fat.

Rusty tried to smile and said, "I'm happy, too. But where's Zeke?"

Lo Fat replied excitedly, "Lo Fat in kitchen, see donkey, over there. Hear gun shoot! Maybe robber come, shoot Lo Fat. Take donkey, gold, everything. So, Lo Fat hide."

Rusty replied, "I sure don't blame you for hidin', Lo Fat, but what happened to Zeke?"

Lo Fat gestured for Rusty to follow him. "Little donkey hide. Lo Fat hide, same place. Come see."

Lo Fat led the way as Rusty and Lee followed him to his little house, located just two streets behind the hotel. As they approached, Rusty's anxiety grew. He looked around the yard but could not see Zeke anywhere.

Lee pointed to the house. "Look! Zeke not hide proper!"

Rusty peered over at the house and then began to laugh so hard his sides hurt. There in the bedroom stood Zeke with his head sticking out of the window. "Zeke! You ornery little cuss!" Then he turned to Lo Fat, "I sure hope he didn't chew up your curtains."

Lo Fat smiled. "No matter curtain. Save donkey! Save gold! Better."

As the happy little group walked back to the hotel, Rusty

looked Zeke over carefully and patted him on the neck. His whole world had changed again. People weren't so bad after all, and gold wasn't cursed. Zeke had once again managed to remind Rusty of how much more important a friendly and loyal animal could be than money. Rusty affectionately patted him again as he mumbled, "It sure is amazing what a big difference a little donkey can make!"

It made Lo Fat happy to see Rusty smiling again. When Lo Fat was happy, he was happy like no one else. His full, round cheeks gave him his unique smile. Everyone who saw him couldn't help feeling that as his eyes smiled shut, his heart smiled open. Further, Lo Fat's smiles and good spirits were contagious. Sometimes just his very presence was enough to cheer up a gloomy situation.

When they arrived at the hotel, Rusty realized that the night's work had made him hungry. He suggested that they have a good breakfast and said to Lee, "Why don't we eat inside? That big dinin' room ain't busy this early in the morning."

Lee hesitated uncomfortably. Then Rusty realized why and said, "Don't — never mind! I guess it's a lot cooler out here anyways."

Rusty remembered that about six months before, Wong Kee, a wealthy Chinese man from Barstow, California, had come to Rhyolite to meet with his friend, Death Valley Scotty. When Wong Kee wanted to eat lunch, none of the cafés or restaurants in Rhyolite would serve him. A "Chinaman" was not welcome in town. So Scotty bought some food in a store, and he and his friend Wong Kee sat right down in the middle of the street in front of the Cook Bank Building and ate lunch. A big crowd gathered, and many people were ashamed that their neighbors had refused to serve these men. Rusty guessed Lee was refusing to eat inside the restaurant for the same reason.

Lee and Rusty sat down on the back steps and talked about the morning's exciting events. Rusty praised Lee for hobbling the horses and told him that was the main reason they had been able to capture the robbers. Lee was especially happy about rescuing Jamie's pony, Beans. Lo Fat soon appeared with a huge stack of pancakes, fried eggs, and a bowl of rice. While they ate, the sun appeared over the mountain and bathed the valley in golden light.

After they finished breakfast, Rusty asked Lo Fat, "Can I get Lee to give me a hand with this here load I'm takin' to Wells Fargo?"

Lo Fat looked puzzled. "Lee, give hand?"

Rusty laughed. "Well, what I mean is give *help*."

Lo Fat smiled as he understood and proudly replied, "When Lo Fat say 'busy, busy,' Rusty help Lee. Now Rusty say 'busy, busy.' Lee help Rusty, okay?"

Lee was glad to help. He carried the sacks and bags of gold into the Wells Fargo Office, while Rusty unpacked the load and stood guard. When they finished the job, Rusty patted Lee on the shoulder and said, "One of these days I'm gonna give you a bag of lucky rice. The durn rice might even be solid gold!"

Rusty had never had a strong urge or the means to help anyone financially. Now he had a chance and something to do it with — his gold. His growing admiration for Lee gave him good reason to think about it.

When Rusty walked into the Wells Fargo Office, Mr. Kimbel was shaking his head in disbelief at the pile of gold Lee had carried in. Greeting Rusty with a firm handshake and a pat on the shoulder, Mr. Kimbel said, "Good to see you, Rusty. Sheriff Tucker was here before sunup. He told me all about the robbery the two of you stopped."

Rusty grinned self-consciously. All he could say was, "Well, uh. . ."

Laughing, Mr. Kimbel asked, "Sure you want to put any more gold in a Wells Fargo with a broken window?"

Rusty looked at the shattered glass on the floor. "I don't guess it matters much where I put it. Two robbers tried to steal my gold 'fore I got it here, and now three robbers tried to get it after it's in the Wells Fargo." Rusty looked out of the window toward the saloon across the street. "You know, this town's gettin' so a feller with a gold tooth better not sleep with his mouth open."

Laughing, they turned their attention to the bags of gold on the big table next to the vault.

Mr. Kimbel weighed the third load and valued it at $36,000, bringing the total value of pure gold in Rusty's account to $78,000.

"This whole gold strike of yours is so unbelievable that news of it has leaked out all over town. I hate to tell you this, but Sheriff Tucker wants to see you before you leave again," said Mr. Kimbel.

Rusty looked surprised. "I'll be needin' a few hundred bucks from my account for some more supplies. Then I'll see the sheriff for sure. I might need a little help to keep from gettin' robbed."

When Rusty left the Wells Fargo Office, he found Big Jim and Ernie, the two men who had been trying to trail him, were back in town. Big Jim was trying to lift Zeke off the ground.

Rusty said, "Hey there! Whaddya tryin' to do? Steal my donkey?"

Big Jim grinned and said, "Naw, just wanted to see if I could lift him."

Just then, a Paiute Indian stepped up, patted Zeke on the rear and asked, "Real live donkey?"

Annoyed, Rusty said, "Sure, he's a real live donkey. Maybe he's full of oats, but he sure ain't no stuffed animal."

The Indian may have smiled inside, but he didn't let it show. Rusty watched the Indian for a moment. He had long, black hair and a strong, handsome face. His big black cowboy hat had a large feather fastened to the band at an odd angle, and his crumpled pants looked almost as worn as his old moccasins. He had no shirt but wore an open buckskin vest, which hung loosely from his shoulders. Without saying another word, the Indian turned and walked back down the street.

Rusty asked the two fellows who were still looking at Zeke, "Ain't that Charley Catch'um, the Paiute feller who helps the sheriff track down outlaws and robbers?"

Big Jim answered, "Yep, that's Charley. When he's trailin', he can tell you if the tracks was made two hours, two days, or two weeks ago." He looked Rusty right straight in the eye and said, "Nobody ever fools him with their crazy tricks. When the sheriff sends him out, Charley always gets his man."

Rusty walked slowly and thoughtfully as he led Zeke over to the Porter Brothers' Store. Mr. Porter could hardly wait to talk to Rusty. After a quick hello, he said, "Well, Rusty, you know I been a thinkin' that I'd like to buy a fifty percent interest in your claim, like you once asked me to."

Rusty chuckled and hitched up his pants. "Well, now, trouble is I don't have no claim or nothin' that even looks like a mine. So, like you once told me, 'Fifty percent of nothin' is still nothin'!'"

Mr. Porter laughed uncomfortably and said, "Maybe you already got some pardners out there helpin' you. Huh?"

Rusty's eyes took on that old twinkle as he thought about Mr. Porter's question. If Mr. Porter thought that he had some big tough partners, he would tell everybody in town. If people heard that he had a couple of real tough partners, they would think twice before trying to track him to his gold camp. "Well, as a matter of fact, I do need two pair of the biggest cowboy boots you got, a real big cowboy hat and a couple of boxes of rifle bullets for a 30-30," replied Rusty nonchalantly.

Mr. Porter looked pleased with himself. This was big news. He tried to look casual as he put the big boots and hat on the counter. "Your pardners must be a couple of real big fellers. These are the biggest boots I've got."

Trying to keep a straight face, Rusty said, "Yep, these'll fit 'em. My pardners are big and tough all right, and one of 'em's a real good shot. Why, he could shoot off those suspenders of yours at a hundred paces, and do it so fast that you'd only notice it after your pants fell down."

Mr. Porter's brow furrowed as he looked down at the clips on his bright green suspenders. He then watched Rusty pick out a few more supplies, including four more sponges and four leather saddlebags, and load the items onto Zeke. He knew that miners didn't usually wear cowboy boots and that the rifle bullets couldn't be for Rusty, because he used a pistol. Given all of the gossip and guessing about Rusty and his gold, Mr. Porter was pleased to have some hard facts that he was certain would be of interest to Sheriff Tucker.

CHAPTER TEN

The Dalton Gang

RUSTY LED Zeke down the street from the Porter Brothers' General Store toward the sheriff's office. As he passed in front of the bank, he noticed Charley Catch'um leaning against the wall. Rusty had a strong feeling that Charley's eyes were following him. Rusty turned the corner and waited briefly. When he peeked around the corner, he saw Charley down on one knee in the middle of the street closely examining Zeke's hoofprints and those of his own hobnail boots. Just as Rusty had suspected, the sheriff had asked this expert Indian scout to track him to his camp and his gold. Rusty had heard that the Indian's real name was Chala Kachim, but most people in Rhyolite called him Charley Catch'um. The sheriffs in Tonopah and Goldfield often used Chala Kachim to track outlaws, and every time he brought one in he proudly announced, "Charley catch 'um!"

Rusty looked at his partner and said, "Well, Zeke Dalton, looks like we gotta figger a new way to outsmart the sheriff and that Paiute feller." They stopped by the kitchen of the Southern Hotel to see Lo Fat and Lee. Rusty thanked Lee for his help that

79

morning and said that he wanted to eat dinner with him that night and do a little "talk-talk."

After a half-hour or so, Rusty went over to the sheriff's office. As he was tying Zeke to a post, Sheriff Tucker and Mr. Porter came out on the boardwalk. Mr. Porter sheepishly tipped his hat to Rusty. After saying good-bye to Mr. Porter, the sheriff turned to Rusty and said, "You're just the feller I wanna see. I wanna talk to you 'bout all this here pure gold you been bringin' to town."

"And I'm a wantin' to see you, too, Sheriff. A couple of fellers robbed me the other day. They got my two canteens full of sand."

Sheriff Tucker laughed softly and said, "Yeah, I heard all 'bout that. Them two fellers boarded the train here. Seems they got to drinking and bought sandwiches and drinks for everybody on the train. Then, when it came time to pay up, all the gold they was braggin' 'bout turned out to be nothin' but sand. They were throwed off the train in Tonopah, and Sheriff Hennessy locked 'em up."

Rusty laughed. "I'm sure glad to hear them fellers didn't miss their train!"

The sheriff became serious again and said, "Now, 'bout this here pure gold you been bringin' in, where you gettin' it from?"

Rusty answered slowly, "Well, sheriff, there's an old saying, 'Gold is where you find it.'"

"Well, where you finding it? You got no claim recorded," asked the sheriff impatiently.

Just then, Big Jim and Ernie walked up to join the conversation.

The sheriff continued. "I checked with the fellow in the assay office, and he told me your gold must've been panned. There ain't enough water 'twixt here and Death Valley to wet your whistle. So whaddya pannin' with, whiskey?"

The fellows laughed when Rusty said, "Maybe I'm just pannin' it with a pan."

Becoming stern, the sheriff continued, "Me and the boys here, Big Jim and Ernie, got to thinkin'. It looks to us like you must be stealin' that gold, 'cause you've got more pure gold than anybody could pan, even if he had lots of water."

Without batting an eye, Rusty answered, "Now if I was to steal gold from a bank, I'd be takin' the gold out, but I been puttin' gold into the Wells Fargo. You know, Sheriff, you must've pinned your badge on crooked when you got up this mornin'!"

The sheriff's face was turning red with anger. "I didn't say you was robbin' a bank. But you must be stealin' it somehow from somewhere!"

Rusty continued in a calm voice, "Now, Sheriff, if I was to steal almost $80,000 worth of gold from somebody, wouldn't you think they might notice it sooner or later and be right over here tellin' you all 'bout it?" The sheriff took hold of his belt with both hands and hitched up his pants. Then he pushed back his hat. He couldn't think of a good reply to Rusty's simple logic.

Rusty turned to Big Jim and Ernie. "Either of you fellers been missin' $80,000 in gold lately?"

The sheriff put his hand on Rusty's shoulder and said, "All we been gettin' outta you is a bunch of smart-alecky talk. Now I want some straight answers. When I found out your name was Dalton, I called Sheriff Hennessy over in Tonopah, and he got all excited. He said he took two pictures of the Dalton Gang before they broke outta jail. He says they never did get pictures of the father and the older brother, but he knows for a fact that the Dalton Gang pulled off more gold robberies than any other gang in the whole West."

Rusty listened to the sheriff's story with increasing amusement. "Now, Sheriff, you know that there's a whole big bunch of Daltons everywhere in this country. If you was to arrest every one of 'em, you sure couldn't fit 'em all in jail. And you'd soon find out they ain't all runnin' 'round in gangs neither."

Big Jim, who was thinking hard about all of this, butted in and said, "Yeah, but the *real* Dalton gang was in this neck of the woods, stealin' gold! You're a Dalton with a lotta gold, and you ain't gonna get away with sneakin' it into town for safe keepin'!"

Grateful for Jim's help, the sheriff agreed. "The three robbers I jailed this morning was real mad that I locked 'em up and let you and the rest of the Daltons get away."

Even more amused, Rusty said, "Get away? Who got away? I'm standin' right here, ain't I?"

"Now look, it takes a lot of guts and real experience for a feller with a pea shooter like yours to hold off three big toughs with rifles. You didn't learn that lookin' under rocks for gold! Sheriff Hennessy's coming down here from Tonopah in a week or so. He asked me to shoot some pictures of you to compare to the Dalton Gang pictures he's bringin' along."

Sheriff Tucker motioned with his arm, and the town photographer, carrying a load of photographic equipment, came out of the sheriff's office. Then the sheriff said, "If you'll just step over here, we need a picture of you out in the sunlight, front and side views."

The photographer worked out his exposure times and took the pictures quickly.

Then the sheriff said, "Now, just to make sure we got a Dalton from the Dalton Gang, we gotta have one more picture with your beard all shaved off." He motioned again, and the barber stepped out of the sheriff's office with a box of shaving gear. "Now, Mr. Dalton, if you'll just sit down on the steps, Dave here will give you a free shave."

Rusty chuckled. "Well now, this is a real occasion. This is the first picture I've had taken since I was nine years old, and the first shave in 'bout twenty years!"

After the shave and the last picture, Rusty took a hand mirror from the barber and inspected his work. "Hmmm, not bad. You know, Sheriff, I might've had a little gold dust in my beard. Mind if I pan them whiskers that the barber shaved off?"

Sheriff Tucker's face grew red with anger again. "Here you go again with them smart-alecky cracks. One of my deputies is gonna take you over to the district mining office, where you'll either file a claim or else be arrested for takin' gold from government land."

Rusty thought a minute and said, "Sheriff, if these fellers out prospectin' for gold find it, do you 'spect 'em to leave it right where they find it? Nobody would be out lookin' for gold at all, if that's how the law worked."

The sheriff's face grew even redder as Rusty continued. "Is there some durn law says a feller can't find pure gold in the desert and bring it to town for safe keepin' in Wells Fargo's safe?"

Sheriff Tucker took a deep breath and replied in a gruff voice, "Now, Mister Dalton, let me tell it to you straight. Mr. Porter from the store was over to see me. He says you got yourself some pardners, big guys who wear big cowboy boots, not miners' boots. You bought some saddlebags, which are for horses, not donkeys. Your pardners use rifles, and Porter says one of 'em is a good shot. You even purchased yourself a pistol and a holster. Ain't nobody packs a gun 'round here no more. This sure sounds like the Dalton Gang to me!"

CHAPTER ELEVEN

The Valley of Ghosts

As RUSTY AND ZEKE walked to the district mining office with the sheriff's deputy, Rusty happened to look back and, sure enough, Charley Catch'um was going into the sheriff's office. Rusty knew right then that he and Zeke would have to do some pretty fancy planning to avoid being tracked. It would take some doin' to outsmart Charley Catch'um.

Rusty filed the claim for his so-called gold mine. The man in charge of the district mining office told him that he would have to send the claim to the county court house in Tonopah to be recorded.

He also told Rusty to make a big pile of rocks as a monument at the site of his mine. To establish legal possession of the seventy-square-acre claim site, Rusty would have to leave a written notice, describing the claim, under a big rock on top of the pile. Rusty was a little hazy about marking the exact site of his mine on the map, so he said, "Well, when I get through piling up them rocks, everybody'll be able to see Mt. Dalton from a couple of miles away."

Rusty was glad that the claim could not be recorded immediately because it would delay anyone from getting back to the site before he did. Anyone else would still have to follow his trail to find his gold. After leaving the district mining office, Rusty and Zeke walked over to take a nap in the shade behind the Wells Fargo Office.

About 7 o'clock that evening, Zeke began nibbling on the toes of Rusty's boots. When Rusty woke up, he yawned and stretched and said to Zeke, "Well, Zeke Dalton, dunno if I was dreamin' or thinkin' in my sleep, but a scheme come to me about how you can outsmart that Charley Catch'um. First, here's your bucket and some oats so's you'll leave my boots alone. Now, just listen to this.

"Seems like years and years ago, some story got started by the Paiute Indians that the ghosts of all the people who died in Death Valley, whether they were Indians, miners, covered wagon folks or outlaws, jump outta their graves on moonlit nights. The ghosts fly right over the Funeral Mountains to a valley like where our camp is. They play-wrassle and even fight for fun. Death Valley is so durn hot the spirits come over to the Valley of the Ghosts. The Paiute Indians ain't zactly sure where this here valley is, but they ain't 'bout to go lookin' fer it."

Rusty laughed as he put his arm around his little pardner's neck and said, "How'd you like ta be the first donkey ghost whatever hee-hawed?"

Rusty needed a few things in order to carry out his plan to outsmart Charley Catch'um. He bought a new hat and a pair of socks at the Porter Brothers' Store. He folded his old hat and tucked it away in the pack on Zeke's back. Then he went to Joe Wilson's corral. Rusty wanted to buy an old, beat-up bridle and lead rope that were hanging on one of the fence posts, but they were in such bad shape that Joe wouldn't take any money for them. Rusty tucked them into the pack also.

Then Rusty and Zeke went to the back steps of the Southern Hotel. Lee came out with a plate of food while Lo Fat watched from the kitchen doorway. They hardly recognized Rusty without his beard.

Rusty smiled and felt his chin with one hand. "Well, I guess you can see that I had a close shave today, but I didn't get cut."

Lo Fat said, "Now Rusty a — a little boy!"

They all laughed, but Lee interrupted, "My fatha mean, now you not look old anymore."

Lo Fat held the door open and said, "I make special table, you, inside, okay?"

Rusty sat down on the steps next to Lee and replied, "Naw, I'll eat out here where me and Lee can talk."

Lo Fat was a little puzzled because Rusty had insisted on paying the full price for all of his meals on the back steps. "People say, 'Rusty rich.' Rich man eat outside?"

Rusty had never been described like that before. "Well, Lo Fat, one thing 'bout bein' rich is, you don't have to try to be somethin' you ain't, and I ain't no bigwig!"

Even more puzzled, Lee asked, "Bigwig? I nevuh hear bigwig!"

Rusty explained that bigwigs are the fellows who wear fancy clothes, derby hats, shiny, black shoes, smoke big cigars, and have wine with expensive dinners.

Lo Fat smiled. When he got the whole idea, he said, "'merican people, funny people!"

While Rusty ate his dinner with Lee on the back steps, he described in detail his scheme to outsmart Charley Catch'um. Then he asked Lee if he could do a few things to help him when he arrived in town with another load of gold. Lee laughed when he heard the plan and eagerly agreed to help Rusty.

In order to carry out Rusty's plan, Zeke had to become

familiar with Lee because they would have to practice doing some things together. So Rusty had Lee start out by holding Zeke's bucket of oats. Lee and Zeke practiced and practiced that evening. Lee surprised Rusty by how well he handled Zeke. Rusty just hoped that Zeke wouldn't eat his weight in oats before it was all over.

The next morning, while Lee and Zeke were practicing, Rusty dropped by to see the sheriff again. This time he walked into the sheriff's office and had a sit-down meeting. Rusty said, "Sheriff, I just wanna 'splain to you 'bout the Dalton Gang."

The sheriff looked a little surprised. "Everything we know 'bout you sure points to that gang. With all that gold you got over at Wells Fargo, we ain't 'fraid of your skipping out."

Now that the sheriff and Mr. Porter were convinced that he was part of the Dalton Gang, the news would spread fast. Rusty wanted the rumor to spread because it would give him even greater protection from outlaws and robbers. The gang connection also gave him another idea that seemed worth a try.

Rusty knew that if he offered his cooperation and good word, the sheriff would agree to his idea. "Well, Sheriff," he said slowly, "I can see that you're thinking straight, so I got an idea here for you."

The sheriff replied, "Okay, just so's it ain't no more of your smart-alecky talk."

Rusty continued. "I filed a claim, and I'm goin' back out to my camp to pile up a rock monument. The gold in my claim is about played out so my next trip might be my last. If I can get my last load of gold safe to town, I guarantee you I can get the Dalton Gang to march right up Golden Street, stop in front of your office and surrender!"

The sheriff was surprised and exclaimed, "Surrender? You mean surrender with no shootin', no rough stuff?"

"Yep, but they won't come outta hidin' and surrender 'til our load of gold is in Wells Fargo's safe, and I give 'em the signal."

The sheriff became a little skeptical. "How do I know that I can depend on you?"

With that twinkle in his eyes, Rusty replied, "Sheriff, it's just like you said. All our gold is tied up here in town at the bank, just in case somethin' was to go wrong. Did ya ever hear of a robber tryin' to 'scape from his own gold?"

The sheriff pushed his hat back a little further. "Now that makes more sense, but I'm still a little leery. Just the other day, I heard some feller say, 'Nobody ever outsmarted that Zeke Dalton.' I never heard of him. Is he part of the gang?"

Rusty replied slowly. "Let's see here. There's four of us Daltons: Hank, Jack, Zeke, and Rusty — that's me. We might not be the Daltons the sheriff in Tonopah is talkin' 'bout, but we'll be here and you fellers can figure out if we're the same gang as the pictures he's got."

The sheriff puffed out his chest. "I don't mind tellin' you that we'll be ready. I'm gonna have men on the roof of the Cook Bank Building, the Overbury Building, and the Porter Brothers' Store. Each of them will have a loaded rifle, just in case."

This precaution pleased Rusty. It gave him a good chance to make his point. "I'm glad to hear y'say that, Sheriff. You know, I had two fellers trailin' me once but they lost our tracks. I had two other fellers hold me up, and they stole my sand by mistake. So y'see, I kinda need your help."

The sheriff asked abruptly, "How's that?"

Rusty continued. "Like I said, if I haul my last load of gold safe to town, everything's gonna work out. If I get robbed, the Dalton Gang will scatter, and there might be some shootin'."

The sheriff looked a little worried. "Well, I might send a couple of my deputies with rifles to meet you and get you to town safe."

By now, Rusty could hardly keep a straight face. "Well, I'll be gol danged. I *never* woulda thought of that! It's the last day 'fore I get to town when I have all the trouble."

The sheriff was proud of the plan that Rusty had carefully led him to propose. "With Sheriff Hennessy coming down here from Tonopah in ten days or so, I sure can't let nothin' go wrong with nabbin' this Dalton Gang," explained Sheriff Tucker. Then he announced boldly, "I'll have my two men with rifles guidin' you safe to town. Just say when and where they gotta be."

The sheriff and Rusty arranged for the two men to meet him at the big rocks across the valley west of town. This would be a short day-and-a-half trip from Rhyolite. Rusty would build a fire when he arrived at the meeting place. The two men would be able to see the smoke from town and would know that Rusty and his gold were there waiting for their escort into town.

Rusty returned to the back of the Southern Hotel and found Lee and Zeke still practicing their little act. Knowing that Lo Fat and Lee would never say a word about his plan made him even more confident. Rusty told Lee about the smoke signal and the sheriff's two horsemen, who would join him at the big rocks, so that Lee could be ready to meet him at the Wells Fargo Office when he arrived in town.

When Rusty finished outlining his plan, Lee became excited and said, "You know man who study rocks?" Rusty shook his head slowly as Lee continued. "Man who say 'gold, no gold, how much gold.'"

Rusty smiled. "Oh, yeah. That's the feller in the assay office."

Lee explained that, when he was clearing tables in the hotel dining room one evening, he overheard the sheriff and the assayer talking at a nearby table. He saw the assayer handing the sheriff a map that showed the location of Rusty's claim. He heard the sheriff say that he would give this map to some of his men and send them to find the claim while Rusty was away making smoke signals. Since the rest of the Dalton Gang would be on their way to town to surrender, no one would be guarding the claim site.

Lee said that the sheriff sounded very pleased. "Sheriff say, 'Plan is perfect. I give you piece of pie.' But I think sheriff not say truth. He not order any pie."

Rusty laughed. "I'll be durned if I don't give *you* a piece of that pie someday. Pie means gold, you know."

Lee looked puzzled, but he laughed when Zeke explained the meaning of "pie."

As Rusty and Zeke left town that afternoon, a group of five horsemen gathered near the schoolhouse. After Rusty passed by, they started to follow him. The men talked and laughed loudly as they slowly walked their horses. Rusty pretended not to notice. After a few minutes, the sheriff came running down the street, yelling and waving his hat. The horsemen stopped, and the sheriff caught up to them. Too breathless to talk, the sheriff just motioned for them to come back to town with him. Rusty grinned and kept plodding along.

What Rusty suspected the sheriff had said to the men proved correct. He had told the men that if they followed Rusty, he would never lead them to his hideout camp and the gold. He would just wander around in the desert until they all ran out of food and water and had to return home. The sheriff also told them that Charley Catch'um was going to track Rusty and would stay far enough behind to be invisible until he found the gold camp. Then everybody would know exactly where the new gold strike was located. This news satisfied the horsemen, so they turned back.

Rusty was relieved that the five men wouldn't be tagging along with him. He had only gone a few more steps when he heard more hoofbeats behind him. As he turned around to check on Zeke, he let out a surprised laugh and beat his hat on one knee. Maude, Rhyolite's pet burro, was just catching up to Zeke. Everybody in town knew Maude.

Rusty smiled. "Well, Zeke, it just goes to show you. When a feller's got a little gold, he gets a lot of new friends real quick." After plodding along for about a mile poor little Maude gave up and turned back toward town.

That evening, Rusty and Zeke crossed the ridge west of town again. "Now, Zeke Dalton, this trip's where you're gonna outsmart Charley Catch'um — the smartest feller the sheriff's got. This time, instead of goin' west from here, we're headin' south to that big, dry lake."

While this route was a little shorter, it was also hotter. Early the third evening, they reached the edge of the dry lake bed, which was three-and-a-half miles wide and perfectly flat. The pure white lake bed was dry as a bone. To the west, Rusty could see the two big peaks of the Funeral Mountains. Their gold camp was on the east slope in the steep ravine between the two peaks. As he looked over this scene in the moonlight, he could see that it was a perfect spot for the Valley of the Ghosts. The ghosts could fly out of Death Valley, over the low mountain pass between the two peaks, and down to their playground — the dry lake.

The Ghosts' Playground

S RUSTY STARTED ACROSS the dry lake, he stopped several times to make sure that his hobnail boots and Zeke's hooves were leaving prints that showed clearly. The dry lake was so smooth and flat that it was a perfect place for anyone to track prints, which fit Rusty's plan perfectly.

Rusty stopped when they were about halfway across the lake to make some changes that would prevent them from leaving any more footprints on the lake surface. While no real footprints would be made, it was possible that a few light marks, like someone walking on his knees, could still show. But on this smooth, chalk white, and slightly dust-powdered surface, a few hours of gentle breeze might erase such traces hinting at a mysterious disappearance. He also scattered a few things around. Then he scuffed up the ground by jumping and kicking his feet in all directions. He vowed to himself that what he did and how he did it would remain a secret until all of his gold was finally safe back in the Wells Fargo vault.

In order to stay out of sight, Charley Catch'um trailed Rusty and Zeke from such a great distance that he did not see them cross the dry lake. He was certain that his great tracking skills would enable him to follow them wherever they might go.

Rusty spent extra time in the moonlight on the dry lake bed, carrying out his plans. When he and Zeke finally reached camp at sunrise, they were tired and hungry.

After a quick drink at the little spring, Rusty fetched the oats and said, "Well, Zeke, I can't get over how a little feller like you puts up with all this here nonsense. But I'll betcha this bucket of oats that we outsmarted old Charley Catch'um."

Rusty knew that Charley Catch'um would follow their tracks easily, and he was sure that Charley would not cross the dry lake in daylight. Anyone could be seen from miles away on that big, white, dry lake. Even at night, in the bright moonlight, he would not be too hard to see.

Rusty decided to take a nap, and he slept until almost sundown. When he awakened, he went to the spring and splashed water on his face. Rusty was amused at how strange the water felt on his face now that his beard was gone. He carefully selected some dry sticks and built a small fire. "I'm gonna warm up some beans and make some coffee. After that, no more fire for us tonight. It might give us away," he told Zeke.

Rusty tied Zeke close to his bedroll at the base of the big boulder overlooking his camp. Then he worked his way up to his lookout spot to see what might be happening far below on the dry lake. His timing was perfect. There, on horseback near the far shore, was Charley Catch'um, just starting to follow their prints across the lake. The full moon was well up in the sky and illuminated the whole desert. Charley Catch'um and his horse looked like actors on a lighted stage.

Charley Catch'um had no trouble following Rusty and Zeke's tracks for the first two miles. Then he stopped suddenly. Rusty chuckled as he watched Charley climb off his horse and bend down on one knee to examine the dry lake surface. All of Rusty and Zeke's footprints ended completely. Leading his horse, Charley walked in a big circle. Rusty knew that no more footprints went out of the circle in any direction. He watched Charley circle back to the spot where he had last seen the prints.

Charley decided to retrace the tracks he had been following and look for prints that might head off in a different direction. This time he walked so he could check more carefully. He found nothing but the same clear prints he had already seen. Still leading his horse, Charley walked back to the center of the dry lake where the tracks disappeared. He had ridden onto the lake bed under a full moon, but now a strange darkness was beginning to appear. He looked up at the moon and stopped abruptly in his tracks. Instead of being pale white, half of the moon was a dark, rustlike color. He hurriedly looked around in the dimming light for any clues to this mystery. He could still see that the smooth lake bed was scuffed up, and it looked like a mighty struggle had taken place on this spot. He leaned over and picked up something and shook the white powdery dust off of it. It was Rusty's old hat! When he looked more closely, he also found two worn socks. An open sack of oats lay next to a beat-up bridle and lead rope. Oats were scattered all around. It was plain to see that Rusty and Zeke had been here, but, somehow, they had both mysteriously disappeared.

Holding Rusty's hat in one hand, Charley stood erect and motionless as he gazed at the dark sky above the pass between the two big mountain peaks. He knew that Death Valley lay just beyond those mountains. He did not guess that he was looking

95

in the direction of Rusty's camp or that Rusty was watching him. Charley's mind whirled. Was this the Valley of the Ghosts? If so, he stood in an evil and forbidden place. He felt certain that Rusty and Zeke must have met with some terrible fate.

❖❖ ❖❖ ❖❖

Watching Charley on the lake bed from his lookout, Rusty also noticed that the cloudless sky was growing darker. More than half of the moon had turned a dark coppery color. Rusty shook his head as he looked up at the moon. He began to wonder if this weird phenomenon was some kind of a sign. Maybe the old Paiute tale of the Valley of the Ghosts was more than just a story. Rusty decided to climb down from his lookout spot before it got any darker.

When he returned to camp, he patted Zeke on the neck and said, "Well, little pardner, I don't wanna get ya all riled up, but, the way things are goin' tonight, I'm not sure who's outsmartin' who!"

❖❖ ❖❖ ❖❖

All but one quarter of the moon was now the mysterious orange color. Charley Catch'um put Rusty's old hat in his saddlebag and looked up at the moon again. Just then, the earth shook with a great jolt. Seeming to jump a foot high, a layer of white dust rose like a mist from the lake bed. Before the dust could settle, another jolt — an audible one this time — shook the earth. The white dust on the lake bed seemed to bounce and shimmer. Along with the heavy tremors, Charley could hear the sound of rocks and boulders crashing down the distant mountain slopes. In this dreadful moment, he became convinced that there was a curse on this forbidden place!

✤✤ ✤✤ ✤✤

Rusty and Zeke huddled close to the base of a large boulder for protection. Big rocks came bounding down the mountain on both sides of their camp. The enormous boulder shook but remained in place. Another sharp jolt sent a landslide of rocks and gravel crashing down on one side of their camp.

Suddenly, a great blow shook the boulder that protected Rusty and Zeke. Rock dust showered them as a huge rock about the size of a stagecoach bounced from the top of the lookout boulder and hit the ground in the exact spot Rusty had used for their campfire. Missing Rusty and Zeke by only a few feet, the gigantic rock bounced again and rolled on down the mountain side, crushing everything in its path.

Trembling, Rusty patted Zeke on the neck and said, "Little feller, while we're still kickin', I gotta tell you somethin'." He paused as he looked up to the heavens and said, "Runnin' around out here in this old desert don't give a feller much of a chance for church-goin', so I'm way behind in my prayin'." He looked back at Zeke. "But, don't let that bother you none, 'cause I'm makin' up for it, all in one night!" Rusty decided that he would never again take Indian stories and legends lightly.

✤✤ ✤✤ ✤✤

Charley Catch'um was deeply disturbed that he had not been able to find Rusty and Zeke. But he wasn't thinking about tracking them anymore. If they were hurt and needed help, it was now too late. These supernatural events had given him a convincing sign. He looked up at the moon. Its entire circle was dimly lit and murky orange in color, but nearby stars glimmered brightly. Charley stood like a stone statue. Then suddenly he became a frenzied mortal who ran like he had just seen the devil himself.

He jumped on his horse, and they raced off at a fast gallop. No horse in the Kentucky Derby ever ran faster than Charley Catch'um's horse that night.

❖❖ ❖❖ ❖❖

It was the longest night Rusty could remember. Aftershocks and sounds of distant rock slides kept him wide awake. He couldn't wait for sunrise. He knew that sunshine wouldn't stop rocks from sliding or rolling down the hill, but at least he would be able to see them coming. At first light, Rusty hustled over to see if the big iron box had moved. He always left the old chest half buried so it would be easy to cover up each time they left camp. It hadn't changed its position during the earthquake.

While Rusty built a fire, he said to Zeke, "If that old box had tipped over and slid halfways down this mountain, we'd be pannin' gold for months." He decided to pack up, rest all day, and then leave camp early the next morning. He filled two of the leather saddlebags with gold, strapped them shut and tied them together so that one bag would hang on each side of Zeke's rump. This would put the weight on Zeke's two hind legs instead of the middle of his back. Each saddlebag of gold weighed about fifty pounds. The rest of Zeke's load would be light because Rusty planned to carry the two canteens of water himself.

Rusty and Zeke left camp by 4:00 the next morning. They knew the route home well and made the trip in record time. When they reached the big boulders, the place they were to meet the sheriff's men a few days later, Rusty placed the two saddlebags of gold between two big rocks. He covered them with sagebrush, perfectly concealing them without disturbing any of the earth or rocks in the area. Then, without a load and not much water, Rusty and Zeke wasted no time in getting started on the return trip to their camp.

❖❖ ❖❖ ❖❖

Charley Catch'um arrived in Rhyolite exhausted from a fast-paced trip. While ashamed of his failure to track Rusty, Charley was clearly agitated about his ghostly experiences. He went into the sheriff's office and stood erect and at attention, like a soldier reporting to his officer-in-charge.

The sheriff greeted Charley eagerly, "You sure got back here quick. You must have spotted his camp real easy."

"I track him prints. I track donkey prints long time. Dry lake, many prints. Then, prints no more," replied Charley.

Charley handed Rusty's old hat to the sheriff. "Him, no more. Donkey, no more. See big fight prints. See donkey rope, many oats. See big cowboy prints, many. No horse print, bad sign."

The sheriff looked puzzled. "Well, that's Rusty's old hat all right, but how could they just disappear into thin air?"

Charley Catch'um replied, "Place. Long time bad place."

After a moment's consideration, the sheriff said, "This sounds like the same story the boys over at the saloon keep tellin' me. They felt like they was trackin' a ghost when they tried to run him down a few weeks ago, and now, big boot prints but no horses!"

By now the sheriff was *really* frustrated. His great scout had failed to find out where Rusty was finding all his gold. And gradually the sheriff's real interest had shifted from protecting or arresting Rusty to getting his hands on some of Rusty's easy gold. But at this point, he would have to be content to help Rusty return to town safely and deposit his gold in the Wells Fargo safe before nabbing the Dalton Gang. Perhaps he could then force them to uncover their mine or stolen treasure.

Although visibly disappointed, the sheriff said, "Charley, I know for a fact that you're the best tracker in this wild country, so I want you on hand when the Dalton Gang gets to town. Maybe the both of us can clear up some of this crazy stuff that geezer and his mule have been up to."

The sheriff had gone far in restoring Charley's dignity, for he didn't think that Charley had failed in his mission. Rather, a great mystery existed that no one could explain.

❖ ❖ ❖

Rusty and Zeke completed the hot trip back to camp. The water in the little spring seemed worth much more than the rest of the gold in the big box. After a good rest, Rusty prepared to make the last trip back to Rhyolite.

He filled the two remaining saddlebags with gold. By the time he had filled four leather bags and the old rice bag with gold, the big iron box was empty. While cleaning up the last of the gold, Rusty found something else that puzzled him. An old piece of wood about a foot-and-a-half long and maybe ten inches wide lay in the bottom of the box. He turned it over and, as old as it was, he could make out the letters LLS FARGO on a faded green background.

His heart sank. If all the gold belonged to Wells Fargo, then he had been doing all of this hard work just to return it to its rightful owner. He sat down and thought about this turn of events. He had planned to simply close the lid on the big iron box, hide it completely with dirt, and then build his rock pile monument on top of it. If he left this old piece of a Wells Fargo strong box inside, no one would ever know about it. The last place they'd probably look would be under the pile with its claim. So he closed the board inside the box, shoveled a fair amount of dirt on top, and gathered some rocks to pile on top of it. Then he stopped, made some coffee, and looked out over the valley, where he could see the dry lake — the ghosts' playground.

Rusty thought of all the things he and Zeke had done to outsmart people and carry the gold safely to town. He remembered how helpful Mr. Kimbel at Wells Fargo had been. It struck him that, although he and Zeke had outsmarted a bunch of people, this was no time to be outsmarted by the gold. Suddenly he jumped up, dumped the rest of his coffee in the fire, took his rusty shovel and cleared the dirt and rocks away from the big iron box. He opened the lid and removed the old wooden board. This board was going back to Wells Fargo with his gold. He wrapped the old green board inside his tattered blanket, then finished building his stone monument on top of the covered iron box, and placed the claim notice under the rock on top. For the first time, Rusty had a clear notion of what he wanted to do with all the gold, and it gave him a sort of warm, golden feeling that he didn't yet fully understand.

CHAPTER THIRTEEN

The Dalton Gang Comes to Town

RUSTY AND ZEKE STOPPED at their little spring for the last time. Rusty washed his hands and face in the cool water. He filled the canteens, had one last drink, then he and Zeke left camp and headed slowly for the big rocks.

As they hiked out, Rusty paused several times to look back at the campsite. The rocky, barren canyon had a stark beauty about it. This place had changed his life. He wondered if he would ever see it again. Zeke carried his 100-pound load once again without any trouble. Other than meeting a few coyotes and jack rabbits along the way, the journey was uneventful. When they finally arrived at the place where the sheriff's two men would join them, Rusty removed Zeke's load, and the two of them rested in the shade. The two saddlebags of gold that Rusty had hidden under some sagebrush were undisturbed. Now he had four saddlebags, two ore sacks, four leather bags, and one rice bag, all filled with gold and ready for the one-day trip to Rhyolite. Rusty decided that it would be safer to take all of the gold in a single trip, rather than in two trips, as he had originally planned.

Rusty built a fire on top of a large flat rock with some fresh white sage and a few old willow sticks he had carried from the gold camp. He knew that the fresh sage would have enough moisture to burn slowly and create a cloud of smoke. When the fire began to smolder, Rusty threw his old blanket over the flames and let all the edges touch the rock. After a moment, he gave the blanket a quick flip upward and a big puff of white smoke rose skyward with the swish of air created by the blanket. Rusty had learned the secrets of making smoke signals from some Shoshone Indians in northern Nevada.

After four or five big white puffs of smoke, Rusty extinguished the fire and prepared another one to signal again in an hour. Grateful for a clear sky and no breeze, Rusty knew that the signals would be visible for many miles. About an hour after sending the second set of smoke signals, Rusty spotted the sheriff's two deputies riding across the valley in his direction.

❖❖ ❖❖ ❖❖

Knowing that they would tolerate no nonsense from Rusty, the sheriff had selected Big Jim and Ernie to be his deputies for this special assignment. As they were riding across the valley, Big Jim, with a sour expression, turned to Ernie and said, "I guess you know that we ain't gettin' no reward for doin' this."

"Yeah, and we might be stickin' our necks out for nothin'!" grunted Ernie.

Big Jim had a thought that cheered him up. "Why don't we check out how much gold he's got and find out where the rest of the gang is." Then, with a crooked, little smile he added, "Maybe we won't need no reward! Look here, Ernie, after we're there awhile, I'll say, 'Ernie, don't you think we oughtta talk turkey!' Then, if things look okay, you say, 'Yep,' and we'll take his gold and git."

Ernie looked surprised, but as the idea slowly sunk in he agreed. "Yeah, that oughtta be duck soup."

Big Jim reminded him, "Now remember, the signal is 'oughtta talk *turkey*,' not duck soup."

✥ ✥ ✥

Rusty did some thinking while he waited. Just what could he do or say if the deputies asked about the rest of the Dalton Gang? He quickly worked out a scheme that involved footprints. He felt confident that his experience at bluffing with tough talk would also help.

When the two deputies arrived about sundown, Rusty had beans and coffee ready for them and was frying some bacon. Big Jim and Ernie were surprised and pleased. They ate and talked with Rusty for awhile.

Finally, Big Jim inquired, "Where's the rest of the Dalton Gang?"

Rusty became suspicious. "They're gonna surrender to the sheriff after the gold's safe in town."

Big Jim sneered. "We know all that! But where's the gang right now?"

Rusty shot right back. "Don't you fellers trust the sheriff?"

"Sure, we trust the sheriff, and he trusts us. So what!" declared Big Jim, acting more and more like a bully.

It was time for Rusty to begin his big bluff. "Well, us Daltons, we don't trust nobody!" Rusty looked Big Jim right in the eye. "But we're a regular bunch. We don't shoot nobody unless they need shootin'." Rusty stood up and pointed down at the ground. "If you're a-hankerin' to know where the Daltons are, just follow their big boot prints, and you'll find 'em."

The two deputies looked closely at the ground around

camp. They were surprised at how big and how deep the cowboy boot prints were in the thin desert soil.

"Sure looks like they're real big fellers, all right!" drawled Ernie meekly.

Rusty interrupted. "'Course, there's a quicker way to find 'em." He pulled out his pistol, whirled it on his trigger finger, and pointed it up into the air. "Just one shot from good old Smokey, and them Daltons will be down here to bury you right on the spot."

The two deputies said nothing.

Rusty turned to Ernie and said, "Your big friend here kinda has it in for me, so maybe you and me oughtta talk turkey."

Both Ernie and Big Jim were startled when Rusty said "talk turkey." They couldn't believe their ears. Could Rusty know about their plan? Rusty quickly realized that something about his question had upset both deputies.

"Not me! How about you, Jim?" replied Ernie meekly.

"Me neither! I don't wanna talk no turkey!" responded Big Jim in a flash.

Rusty laughed. "Well, I always heard that any feller that wouldn't talk turkey must be chicken!"

Rusty was the first one up the next morning. He loaded Zeke's pack and built a small fire. Since the two men had arrived with plenty of water in their canteens, Rusty made some coffee. Having awakened to the smell of coffee, the two deputies were in a good mood and drank their fill. Then Rusty announced, "Well, fellers, I'm ready to load you up for the trip back."

"Load us up?" both men said at once.

"Yep, the sheriff said he'd send you out here to get me and my gold back to town safe," replied Rusty, matter-of-factly. "So

I got brand new leather saddlebags for you. If you just hang 'em on your saddle horns, lettin' one hang down on each side, you got a quick, easy load. I got sponges squeezed in the tops of them saddlebags so's no gold's lost."

"I'll be durned! He didn't say nothin' about our carryin' some of your gold," grumbled Ernie.

Rusty handed a saddlebag to Ernie and said, "Now you wouldn't want to get all them Daltons mad by just leavin' their gold sittin' out here in the desert. An' besides that, the sheriff'ud be madder'n a wet hen."

Ernie agreed. "Well, let's load up. We can handle them saddlebags okay."

Big Jim had a sneaky look in his eyes as he lifted the two heavy saddlebags full of gold and swung them over his saddle horn. "Say, Ernie, don't you think maybe we oughtta talk chicken?"

Ernie, who was confused most of the time, didn't catch on. "Talk chicken?"

Big Jim hurried to correct his mistake. "No, not chicken! I don't mean chicken. I mean turkey. Yeah, turkey, that's it! Maybe we oughtta talk turkey!"

Rusty drew his pistol, whirled it a time or two, and slipped it back into his holster in a flash. He winked at Ernie, whose Adam's apple was jumping up and down.

In a strong but nervous voice, Ernie answered, "Big Jim, you said it right the first time! I don't wanna talk nothin', not even chicken!"

Rusty cut in. "Look, you fellers got the whole trip to town to call each other chicken, so why don't we just get movin'. Gettin' this gold back to town oughtta be duck soup!"

Just then, something hit the ground with a thud, followed by a loud groan. Startled, Big Jim stood up in his stirrups and yelled, "Don't shoot! Don't shoot!"

Rusty, equally as surprised, responded, "I didn't hear no shot!"

Big Jim looked down at the ground and said, "Gol durn it, Ernie, what are you doin' down there on your back?"

Poor Ernie had been so nervous when he loaded up that he had hung both bags of gold over the same side of his horse. The unbalanced weight had caused his saddle to slip over to one side. When Rusty mentioned duck soup, Ernie became so upset that he lost his balance and fell off his horse. Groaning in pain from a sprained ankle, Ernie needed help to climb back on his horse.

Rusty couldn't resist this chance to put a little frosting on the cake. "Sheriff Tucker sent you two out here to help me get back to town safe. Now it looks like I gotta help you fellers get back to town instead, safe or not. Maybe us Daltons are gettin' too finicky 'bout who needs shootin'!"

They arrived in town right on time. Lee was waiting outside the Wells Fargo Office, just as he and Rusty had planned. The two deputies carried the heavy saddlebags into Mr. Kimbel's office, while Rusty unloaded the assortment of gold bags that Zeke had carried.

Rusty took his pistol from Zeke's load and strapped the holster around his hips. Then he turned Zeke over to Lee. "You got 'bout a half-hour to get ready. An' remember, no oats for Zeke right now."

No one noticed Lee as he led Zeke around to the back of the Southern Hotel.

A big crowd had gathered in front of the Wells Fargo Office. Rusty thanked the two deputies and told them the new saddlebags would be theirs as soon as they were empty. After they left, Mr. Kimbel locked the front door to his office and said to Rusty, "This whole town's goin' crazy 'bout seein' the Dalton Gang give up. You sure know how to get yourself into a pickle."

Rusty just smiled and opened one of the four saddlebags. The gold in it weighed just over fifty pounds.

After weighing all the gold, Mr. Kimbel figured that this last load had a value of $63,100. This brought the total of Rusty's gold account to $141,100. "That's a whopping pile of gold you've got locked up in our safe, and it's beginnin' to worry me. I see you've even started wearin' a gun around town. We really ought to ship your gold out of here to that mint in San Francisco, before our safe is robbed or you get shot."

Rusty chuckled. "Well, Mr. Kimbel, I gotta few things we oughtta chew the rag about, soon as I get the Dalton Gang to surrender."

Rusty loosened his holster belt a notch so that it hung low on one side like a gunslinger's. His old beard had given him the look of an old prospector, but the stubble he had grown since his shave nearly ten days ago made him look like a real outlaw. He pulled his hat down lower in front than he usually wore it.

When Mr. Kimbel unlocked the front door, Rusty walked out with a bold stride. "Well, Mr. Kimbel, I'll be a seein' you soon as I take care of the sheriff!"

There must have been at least 200 people standing in the street. Those who were close enough to hear what Rusty had said to Mr. Kimbel were shocked. Rusty looked tough. They had always thought of him as a harmless, friendly, old fellow, but now they could see that this Dalton Gang was for real. Most folks thought that their sheriff had played it right. He let that innocent-looking ol' Rusty sneak a lot of their gold right into the Wells Fargo vault before he closed in on the gang. The word spread fast, and the crowd grew. That gang of vicious bandits had been tricked into a trap where they would have to surrender.

With long, deliberate strides, Rusty walked slowly up Golden Street toward the sheriff's office. The crowd had grown. Now, more than 300 people lined both sides of the street. Rusty looked up at each of the sheriff's men, holding rifles and standing on top of the three biggest buildings in town. The people in the street looked up, too, and fear started to grip the crowd. Children ran to hide behind their mothers' skirts.

Sheriff Tucker stepped off the boardwalk in front of his office, took off his hat, and waved it at the crowd. "Now, I want everybody off the street, back against the buildings, and up on them boardwalks. There ain't supposed to be no shootin' here today, but fellers who belong to these dangerous gangs don't always keep their word."

Rusty continued his slow, deliberate stride. A showdown between Rusty and the sheriff seemed unavoidable. People lined the boardwalks up and down Golden Street. The crowd was perfectly silent, as if everyone were holding their breath. Not even a dog barked.

The sheriff took another step forward as Rusty came to a halt in front of his office. "Mr. Dalton, in the name of the law, I place you under arrest!"

One of the sheriff's deputies moved in quickly to handcuff Rusty. The sheriff waved him off. "Jake, you can forget them handcuffs. We finally got this old desert rat in a trap where he's done for." The sheriff turned back to Rusty. "Just so's you'll know, Mr. Dalton, this is Sheriff Hennessy and Judge Hodges from Tonopah. And here is our own good mayor of Rhyolite,

Mr. Simpson. Our photographer is here to document this occasion, and Charley Catch'um will verify footprint evidence."

Rusty tipped his hat to the distinguished group of visitors and officials. "Well, I'm real happy to meet all you fine fellers, but what in the name of the law am I gettin' 'rested for?" Sheriff Tucker spoke up quickly. "Sheriff Hennessy's got pictures here of two members of the Dalton Gang and, comparin' your picture with theirs, it's easy to see you're one of 'em."

Rusty countered with, "You mean I'm gettin' 'rested just for looking like some other feller?"

Sheriff Hennessy handed Rusty one of the photos of the Dalton Gang and said, "Just look at those eyes, that nose, and even the ears. You're a dead ringer for this guy."

Sheriff Tucker added, "Can't you see the resemblance?"

Rusty said, "Let me see here," as he took the picture and looked at it more closely. A smile spread across his face as he responded slowly. "Well, yeah . . . this feller in the picture has two eyes, two ears, and one nose. Same as me!"

Sheriff Tucker grew angry. "Like I was sayin', Judge Hodges, this ol' fool is always comin' up with them smart-alecky remarks." Then in a loud, clear voice the sheriff said to Rusty, "Signal your gang to come out of hiding and surrender."

Rusty chuckled. "Well, Sheriff, I gotta walk up Golden Street just past the Southern Hotel, so's they can see me and hear my signal. Tell them fellers on the rooftops to hold their fire till my signal gets heard."

The sheriff replied, "Well, if you gotta signal 'em, it's okay, but I have to tell you I got one of my deputies on horseback with a rifle on the south end of town and another on the north end of town. There's no way you're gonna outsmart the good citizens of Rhyolite."

It wasn't hard to see that Sheriff Tucker enjoyed making speeches to such a big crowd and demonstrating that he was a top-notch lawman.

"Sheriff, like I said, I'm kinda honored to meet our mayor and these fellers from Tonopah, so now I'm gonna introduce the Dalton Gang to everybody," said Rusty.

Taking big strides, Rusty turned and walked slowly up Golden Street. When he was about half a block from the far end of the Southern Hotel, he stopped. Then he turned and faced the street lined by crowds on both sides. He looked up at the armed men on the rooftops. Keeping an eye on everyone, he slowly walked backwards. To people in the crowd, it looked as if the Dalton Gang might try to break out of this big trap and make a run for it.

Rusty took a few more slow steps backwards and quickly drew his ivory-handled pistol from the holster. He twirled it around on his trigger finger and slid it back into the holster like a real gunslinger. Rusty had practiced this trick for hours at the camp.

The crowd was tense. One woman fainted, and several children were crying. After a few more slow steps backwards, Rusty heard the clang of Zeke's oat bucket as Lee's arm reached out and put it down by the corner of the building. Rusty stopped, stared up the street at the sheriff and the crowd of people, and then drew his gun again. He fired two quick shots into the air. After a second or two, he fired a third shot. Women screamed, dogs barked, children cried, and men froze in their tracks. The men on the rooftops took aim at Rusty with their rifles, but held their fire.

Rusty calmly blew the smoke away from the muzzle of his gun and slid it back into its holster. The signal, three loud shots, had been given. The Dalton Gang would soon come out of hiding.

Rusty pulled his hat down a little lower. Then, with his right hand firmly on the ivory handle of his pistol, he picked up the bucket left by Lee with his other hand and started down the street. Slowly, but bravely, he approached the sheriff's office.

With rifle in hand, Sheriff Tucker stepped off the boardwalk, away from his office, and walked into the center of the street. Rusty started walking toward him slowly.

The crowd grew quiet again. Everyone could see that this was going to be a real shoot-out!

CHAPTER FOURTEEN

When All the Chips Are Down

ITHOUT LOOKING BACK, Rusty walked steadily down Golden Street toward the sheriff. He was taking a big gamble, but some kind of inner confidence kept him going. When Rusty had heard Lee bang on the bucket of oats, he knew that Lee had led Zeke around the corner as planned. Zeke was wearing a pair of big cowboy boots on his hind legs and another pair on his front legs. On his head was a big cowboy hat with two holes cut out for ears. Without a lead rope, Zeke followed Rusty, who continued down the street without looking back. The crowd watched with growing disbelief. The children came out of hiding and began to giggle. Some people in the crowd began to titter, others laughed openly. The laughter moved through the crowd like an ocean swell, and soon everyone was roaring.

Keeping a straight face, Rusty continued his deliberate pace with Zeke plodding along behind until he reached the front of the sheriff's office, where all of the notables were standing. Then Rusty unbuckled his holster and, with the pistol still in place, threw it down on the ground in front of the sheriff as a token of surrender. By now the whole valley seemed to shake with laughter.

Zeke had followed along behind Rusty all the way from the far corner of the Southern Hotel, past the Cook Bank Building and down Golden Street. He stopped behind Rusty in front of the sheriff's office.

This turn of events prompted a spontaneous outburst of relief from the crowd. Only moments ago, a shoot-out seemed almost a dreadful certainty. Now, the crowd was being treated to a rip-roaring comedy act that was better than anything they'd seen in the big city. People moved away from the crowded storefronts and boardwalks to form a circle around Rusty and Zeke, who stood in front of the sheriff's office.

Sheriff Tucker was mighty embarrassed and madder than a hornet. "What's the meanin' of all this nonsense? You, you durned old fool!" he demanded.

Rusty replied calmly. "Maybe, I could 'splain it better if you was to get Charley Catch'um to check out our footprints. You said he was here to verify 'em or somethin'."

Annoyed, the sheriff motioned for Charley Catch'um to check the footprints that had just been left in the soft, dusty street.

Charley dropped down on one knee, examined the prints, and slowly shook his head, saying, "Same. Him prints. Same. Cowboy prints." With a stern look on his face, Charley returned to Sheriff Tucker's side.

Rusty swept off his hat and offered an expansive bow to the sheriff, the notables, and the crowd. "Now, to all you fine fellers from outta town and all you fine folks in town, I want to introduce the Dalton Gang."

He pointed to Zeke's hind legs. "These boots back here made Hank Dalton's footprints." Then he pointed to Zeke's front legs. "These boots up front here made Jack Dalton's footprints.

As you all know, I'm Rusty Dalton, and my prints are from these here hobnail boots."

Rusty pulled up his pants and waved his hat at the crowd. "An' now, the leader of the gang, Zeke Dalton! He's the feller here with the hat on."

The crowd roared with laughter. By the time they finally calmed down, Sheriff Tucker's face was fiery red. "You mean to say *this* is the Dalton Gang?"

Rusty proudly replied, "Yep," and winked at the crowd. "Now, if you want to compare the pictures Sheriff Hennessy has of the Dalton Gang, you can see a definite resemblance or whatever you call it. Notice how Zeke here has two eyes, two ears, and one nose, just like all them other Dalton fellers."

Both sheriffs were caught off guard and couldn't think of anything to say. Rusty motioned to Mr. Gottschalk, the photographer, to come closer. "Now's your chance to snap some real good pictures of Zeke Dalton. You want to take 'em before and after we give him a shave, front and side view, and all that stuff?"

This time, it took a full two minutes for the crowd to quiet down. The sheriff regained his composure and looked squarely at Rusty. "This is just a bunch of your smart-alecky talk again. I thought you knowed better than that!"

"Sheriff Tucker, I promised you the Dalton Gang would surrender, and I kept my word," replied Rusty.

The sheriff snapped back, "You and that stupid donkey ain't no gang, and you know it!"

Rusty smiled and asked, "Well, then, how come we got arrested in the name of the law?"

The crowd tittered, and the sheriff's face grew red again. He was losing his patience. "That's enough of your nonsense. Now, what I want to know is how you disappeared from that dry lake a couple of weeks ago. We know you was there. I've got your old hat right here to prove it."

Rusty smiled as the sheriff handed him his old hat. Then he looked around at the crowd and scratched his head. He dropped his old hat on the ground and slowly said, "Well, Sheriff Tucker, you and these folks here might not believe this, but here's what we did."

Rusty patted Zeke on the neck while he thought about exactly what he was going to say next. Then that old twinkle appeared in his eyes. "We left my hat and some other stuff lying on the dry lake to prove we was there, like you said. Then Zeke and me walked backwards, puttin' our feet in the same prints we made coming out on the dry lake. Our prints was easy to see, you know. We walked backwards all the way till we was off the lake bed where we came in."

The sheriff grinned, feeling certain he had finally caught Rusty in a lie. "Now, that's a real whopper if I ever heard one! Do you expect me and all these folks out here to believe that?" He removed his hat and waved it at the crowd and said, "How would all you folks here like to see Dalton and that stupid donkey walk backwards in their own footprints?"

The crowd laughed and cheered. This was more fun than a circus! They knew that the sheriff had Rusty trapped this time. But Rusty just smiled and said, "Nothin' to it. Course Zeke ain't so good at it when he's wearing his boots. But here goes, anyway."

Though Rusty and Zeke had practiced this walking backwards trick many times, they could never do it well enough to fool anyone tracking them. But Rusty knew that they could do it well enough to have some fun and entertain the crowd. He stood four steps ahead of Zeke, who stood still and looked at Rusty's back. Rusty took four slow, deliberate steps backwards until he was even with Zeke's head. After a pat on his neck, Zeke started to follow along with Rusty. They walked backward, side-by-side, for six or eight steps and stopped. The crowd cheered and applauded.

Dumbfounded, the sheriff was madder than ever. He could see that everyone really believed Rusty's crazy story about walking backwards. He had an uneasy feeling that, for him, this day was turning from triumph to ruin. He glanced at Judge Hodges, who shot back a look of irritation.

When the crowd settled down again, Rusty said, "You know, Sheriff Tucker, there's more than one way to skin a cat. So, we'll show you another way of disappearin.'"

The sheriff disregarded that remark and resumed his interrogation, "Now, Rusty, Charley Catch'um tells me that, as he was trackin' you, the footprints disappeared. How do you explain that?"

Rusty stood up as tall as he could and waved his hat over his head. Lee pushed his way through the crowd to help Rusty with the next trick, which they had practiced together. He carried four empty leather bags, which were used to hold gold dust. Lee and Rusty quickly reached into Zeke's cowboy boots and pulled two sponges from each boot. The sponges had made the boots fit firmly enough to stay on as Zeke walked down Golden Street behind Rusty. Now, Rusty removed the boots from Zeke's legs while Lee forced a sponge into each of the four leather bags. Zeke was very patient as Rusty raised one hoof at a time and placed it into a leather bag. Each hoof bore down on the sponge inside its bag, leaving no room to spare. Lee quickly tied the leather thongs at the tops of the bags around Zeke's legs above his hooves, which made Zeke look like he was wearing big boxing gloves. Rusty and Lee finished at the same time, stood up together, and held their arms straight up like the rodeo cowboys do when they've finished calf-roping in record time. The crowd laughed, even though they didn't know what all of this was leading up to.

Switching his heavy hobnail boots for his soft Indian moccasins, Rusty said, "Now, all you good folks know that the dust is so deep on this street that you could see an ant's footprints. Well, out in that ol' desert where a couple of hundred people ain't walking back and forth all day, the ground's crusty and rocky. These fancy footprints that you're gonna see here ain't all that easy to see out there."

Then, Rusty proceeded to walk lightly in his Indian moccasins. And Zeke followed along, wearing his soft spongy bags as shoes. It was surprising how faint their tracks were as they walked a few steps. Charley Catch'um came forward to inspect the new tracks. Big Jim and Ernie, who had first tried to trail Rusty, stepped forward to see the trick that had made them think they were following a ghost. They shook their heads, not really knowing what to believe anymore.

Big Jim turned to Ernie and hissed under his breath, "You're the one who said gettin' his gold oughtta be duck soup! You lily-livered chicken!"

Sheriff Tucker was dismayed. He had to salvage the situation somehow. Looking at the crowd, the sheriff said, "Sorry to spoil your fun, folks, but I'm gonna end all this nonsense. This hokey-pokey circus Dalton's been puttin' on here is just to get us off the track. He's doin' everything under the sun to keep all of us from finding out where he's been gettin' all this gold."

The sheriff smiled expectantly at Rusty as the crowd watched to see his reaction. Rusty smiled, took off his hat, looked it over closely, and then carefully picked a small grain of sand from the brim. He held it up to the light, turned it back and forth, then carefully dropped the "gold nugget" he'd just found into his shirt pocket. The crowd began laughing again as he tipped his hat to them. When he saw the sheriff's determined look, he put his hat back on and stood at attention without smiling. This made the crowd laugh even more.

The sheriff resumed his speech. "Oh, he's tricky all right. He just tricked two of my deputies into carryin' his last load of gold into town. Each one carried over a hundred pounds. That's about $50,000 in gold. Then he tells me his mine is all played out. But his phantom gold mine keeps turnin' out real gold!"

The crowd became quiet. Somewhat regaining his confidence, the sheriff continued, "You can't believe anything Dalton says, so I'm gonna call his bluff right here in front of all you folks."

Sheriff Tucker motioned to Judge Hodges, who handed him some legal papers. The sheriff waved the papers over his head as he addressed the crowd. "Now, I want all you folks to be witnesses to this. I'm offerin' to buy a half-interest in Mr. Dalton's claim for $10,000. If he don't take my offer, you'll know there's still a big pile of gold out there."

Mr. Porter interrupted, "I'll offer $15,000 for a half-interest in his claim."

The sheriff was shaken by this unexpected turn of events, but Mr. Porter's bid increased his confidence in acquiring a share of Rusty's gold. The sheriff continued, "I didn't plan this to be no auction, so Mr. Porter, I wish you'd stay outta this right now. I'm changin' my bid to $20,000." Turning to Mr. Porter, he muttered quietly, "I can cut you in for a piece of this later."

At this point, Rusty interrupted the proceedings and said to the crowd, "Mr. Porter once told me that fifty percent of nothin' is still nothin'. I'm telling all of you that there ain't nothin' left out there where my claim is."

The sheriff smiled as things appeared to be going his way. He handed Rusty a pen. "Well, if fifty percent of nothin' is nothin', you ought to be real glad to sign this paper and make some easy money."

Rusty hesitated. The sheriff continued, "Everybody here's gonna know you're lying if you don't sign."

A few loud remarks from the crowd backed up the sheriff and made Rusty look like a real "no-good." The sheriff held the open ink bottle as the papers were placed on a street railing. Rusty slowly dipped the pen into the ink and signed two copies. Then the sheriff signed both copies, and, obviously pre-planned, Sheriff Hennessy and Judge Hodges signed both copies as witnesses. The notary pressed the official notary seal, completing the contract.

The crowd cheered. The sheriff shook hands with Judge Hodges, Mr. Porter, and Sheriff Hennessy. Rusty looked at his copy of the contract and the $20,000 check that went with it. He handed both to Mr. Kimbel to put in his vault for safe-keeping.

Rusty turned to the crowd and said, "In this town, every time I tell the truth, nobody believes anything I say. Everytime I tell lies, everybody believes everything I say. You know it kinda makes a feller feel good when folks believe what he tells 'em. After my first lie, when everybody believed everything I said, I got to feelin' so good that I've had a hard time tellin' the truth ever since."

Not exactly sure how they should react to this, folks in the crowd murmured, laughed, jeered, and applauded all at once. As the crowd grew silent and slowly started to leave, they suddenly heard two shots!

CHAPTER FIFTEEN

It Ain't Over 'Til It's Over

FOUR OR FIVE MORE SHOTS blared in rapid succession! The sound came from the south end of town, not more than a mile away. The crowd on the street milled about in confusion and yelled as people pressed against storefronts to seek cover. A few men cried out, "It's the real Dalton Gang! The Daltons are a-comin'! Run for your lives!"

The men with rifles, who had been on top of the three big buildings, were now scattered on the ground. The deputy with a rifle, whom the sheriff had stationed at the south end of town, had returned his horse to Joe Wilson's stable.

Three more shots rang out even louder than the first ones. Holding their rifles high in the air, two men on horseback came galloping up the street. They fired two more shots as they continued up the street at a full gallop. Women and children ran inside the stores that would give them entrance. Men disappeared around corners into alleys or into the nearest saloons. The out-of-town dignitaries hurried into the sheriff's office and closed the door. The sheriff grabbed his rifle and stood on the boardwalk in front of his office. Rusty grabbed his holster, which was still lying on the ground in front of the sheriff, and strapped it around his hips. Rusty walked to the middle of the street and bravely faced the fast-charging riders. The people who watched from windows and hiding places were amazed at his bravery.

Rusty did not want to pass up another chance to put one over on the sheriff. From the first shots, he had guessed at what was actually taking place. He remembered Lee's story about the sheriff sending two men out with a map to find his claim. He knew that the expedition was destined to fail.

As the horsemen approached, they were yelling at the same time, garbling each other's message. Just as panic and confusion reached a high point, Rusty pulled out his ivory-handled pistol, whirled it on his trigger finger, and then fired two shots into the air.

The horsemen came to a sudden halt as they yelled again, "Sheriff! Sheriff! Hold everything! Wait, Sheriff! Wait!"

Now the crowd slowly recognized that these were two of the sheriff's own men. The street was soon full of people eager to find out what was going on.

The riders jumped off their horses and approached the sheriff. One of them said, "We rode back here fast as we could 'cause we got bad news."

Looking worried, Sheriff Tucker said, "Didn't you find Dalton's claim?"

The other fellow answered, "Yeah! We found it all right. But there wasn't no diggin's anywhere. No mine of any kind. No gold or nothin'."

Grasping desperately for a shred of hope, the sheriff asked, "Sure you found the right place? Did it have a monument?"

The sheriff's men looked dejected. One of them handed the sheriff a crumpled piece of paper. "Yep, it had a monument all right, and here's the claim notice."

The sheriff stared at the claim notice, which read,

NOTISE

CLAIM JUMPERS

YOUR 1 JUMP TO LATE

Rusty an' the Dalton Gang

By now the sheriff was so red in the face and so mad he could have bitten a spike in two. He turned to Rusty and barked, "You durned old fool! Is that a fact? I'm gonna arrest you for fraudulent sellin' of worthless claims on a phantom gold mine!"

Rusty answered as kindly as he could. "Sheriff, just awhile ago, I told you and all these people standin' here that fifty percent of nothin' is nothin'. I told you this load of gold today was my last trip, that my claim was all played out. As I keep a-saying, whenever I tell the truth, nobody believes anything I say."

The sheriff thought fast in an effort to escape the worthless contract he and Rusty had signed. "What I wanna know is, whaddya gonna do about this trick contract we just signed?" asked the sheriff.

Rusty paused, looked at the crowd, looked at Zeke, and said, "Well, to tell you the truth, this whole thing's kinda like a game us kids used to play years ago. We called it 'Pin the Tail on the Donkey.' But today, it's the other way 'round. Zeke and me have pinned the donkey's tail on you. Fact is we pinned the donkey's tail on this whole danged town!"

So overcome with his own joke, Rusty broke into a wild and boisterous laugh. Then he did his crazy little jig and laughed as gleefully as he had the day he and Zeke discovered their gold.

And sure enough, Zeke stretched his neck, raised his head, and loudly hee-hawed twice, just as though they had rehearsed this act for months. The crowd roared with laughter, and a lot of the kids started yelling, "Hee-haw! Hee-haw!" The sheriff and his distinguished guests didn't think it was so funny. They went into his office and slammed the door.

Charley Catch'um, however, stood silent and erect amidst all of the noise and excitement. He neither laughed nor smiled. No one noticed, because he never smiled anyway. But Charley had a strange look in his eyes as he watched Rusty, Lee, and Zeke walking slowly up the street.

CHAPTER SIXTEEN

Settlin' Up Without Settlin' Down

B Y EVENING, RUSTY was worn out. His day had started at 2 o'clock in the morning and had included a long walk across the desert and a lot of hard work in outwitting the sheriff. He led Zeke down to Joe Wilson's stable and asked Joe to take care of him overnight. Then he walked back up town to the Southern Hotel. Along the way, people smiled, laughed, and said hello to him. This time, he walked right in through the front entrance of the hotel and asked to see the manager. Someone immediately escorted him into Mr. Nelson's office.

The manager stood up as Rusty entered. He walked around from behind his desk, extended his hand, and said, "It's a real pleasure to see you again, Mr. Dalton. I guess you know that you've just become something of a hero in this town?"

Rusty grinned. "Well, I sure don't look like no hero. I'm gonna get a new shirt and some pants and things from Mr. Porter's store. What I wanna do right now is to get a room in your hotel so's I can get cleaned up and rested."

Mr. Nelson smiled and replied, "We are honored to have you as a guest. If there is anything at all that we can do for you, just say the word."

"Tonight I'm so durned tired, I'm gonna try to sleep in a bed, even if it gives me a backache," said Rusty. He paused and then slowly said, "But I want to ask a special favor for tomorrow night. I'll pay for it, an' I want to get the best."

Mr. Nelson smiled and asked, "What is your pleasure, sir?"

Rusty confidently stated his request. "I want a table in your main dinin' room and your best dinner."

Still polite and anxious to please, Mr. Nelson said, "Very good, sir. How many will be in your party, and what time would you care to dine?"

"There's gonna be three, Lo Fat, Lee, and me. And dinnertime is okay," replied Rusty, matter-of-factly.

Mr. Nelson was taken aback but quickly regained his composure. "Mr. Dalton, your request may be a bit difficult to honor. You must already know that Mr. Lo Fat is our chef."

Rusty smiled. "Aw, that oughtta be easy. Lo Fat can cook the dinner, then come in an' sit down with Lee and me. Let them waiter fellers bring the food in."

Mr. Nelson replied, "This is highly irregular, but for such an honored guest, we'll bend the rules and do as you ask." Then Mr. Nelson grew expansive in his acceptance of such a dinner party. "I will say that Mr. Lo Fat is a fine chef. We hired him to come here from San Francisco. Every month he sends money home to his wife and young daughter."

Rusty was surprised to learn this. "Well, whaddya know 'bout that."

Mr. Nelson continued. "He earns more here than he could earn in San Francisco. When he saves enough money, he plans to return and open his own restaurant. So for now, we are very fortunate to have such an excellent chef in our hotel."

As Rusty thanked him and turned to go, Mr. Nelson said,

"Mr. Dalton, if you have some time, I'd like to tell you a few more things about our chef and his son."

Rusty replied, "Well, I guess you already know they're durn good friends of mine."

Mr. Nelson leaned back in his swivel chair. "Yes, I know that. I also know all about the rescue in the big wash. Lo Fat asked me to talk to the sheriff for him if his son didn't return."

Rusty was surprised but pleased as Mr. Nelson went on. "That boy wanted to have a garden. Can you imagine trying to raise anything in Rhyolite's rocky soil?" Mr. Nelson explained that Lee had offered to clean the two bath tubs in the hotel after each use if he could use the soapy water for his garden. He also used the soapy water from the kitchen after the dishes were washed. Lee claimed that soapy water was even better than clear water for his garden. Mr. Nelson said that he was surprised to find out later that the chemicals in soapy water were, indeed, beneficial to plant growth. He then described how Lee dug up his little plot of ground and sifted the rocks out of the soil, added potato peelings and horse manure. Then he added more potato peelings and more manure until the soil was just right.

"Lee had the soil looking like chocolate cake by the time he planted his seeds. That kid performed a miracle. He turned poor soil, potato peelings, horse manure, and soapy bath water into soil that produced the most wonderful tasting watermelons I ever ate," said Mr. Nelson enthusiastically. "Farmers raised vegetables, but no melons, in nearby Beatty. On the bumpy railroad tracks, melons from California would crack and split open before they ever got to Rhyolite."

Then Mr. Nelson smiled and continued, "But the big thing in Lee's mind was that when he put water into the ground, the watermelons gave it back!" Mr. Nelson chuckled and said that he had never known any Chinese people before. However, in spite of some language difficulty, Lee and Lo Fat had a great sense of humor. He continued, "When I asked Lo Fat how his son learned to be such a wonderful gardener, he told me, 'Wise man never plant garden bigger than son able to care for.'"

Rusty and Mr. Nelson had a good laugh. Then Mr. Nelson added, "Seriously, I think that young fellow is going to do something great someday."

"Mr. Nelson, I'm beholden to you for tellin' me all this. You know, them two ain't much for braggin' 'bout the things they do," said Rusty, as he followed the bellhop upstairs.

The bellhop showed Rusty to his room and pointed out a nice bathroom down the hall. Then Rusty walked over to Porter Brothers' Store to buy some new clothes. Dead tired, he returned to the hotel, where he took a bath, chewed some jerky, and fell asleep in his bed without having eaten dinner. About midnight, Rusty awoke with a stiff back. He pulled the blankets from the bed, spread them on the floor, and slept comfortably the rest of the night.

The next morning, Rusty enjoyed eating breakfast in the dining room. He was beginning to feel like a new man, especially when others in the dining room smiled at him and said good morning. Rusty knew that Lo Fat was busy with all of the breakfast orders, so he walked out of the hotel and around to the back steps, where Lee was busily working.

"Hi, Lee, whaddya workin' on so early?" asked Rusty.

"Hotel man say Rusty have big dinner tonight. My fatha and me, too, in dining room," replied Lee with a big smile.

"What is this stuff here?" asked Rusty.

"Shrimp. Very special for tonight."

Rusty looked at them closely and said, "I heard of them things but never ate none."

"You like, and pea pod, too. And my fatha special lucky rice. Big China dinner. My fatha make number one dinner for you."

Rusty could see that plans were already being made for their evening. He was pleased that Lo Fat and Lee were going to sit with him in the dining room. But before he could give any more thought to their dinner, Rusty had some important business to finish.

Rusty returned to his room for the old board he'd found at the bottom of the iron chest of gold. With that in hand, Rusty headed for the Wells Fargo Office. Mr. Kimbel greeted him warmly, "Good to see you, Rusty. Now I 'spose it's time for us to settle up and straighten out a few things."

Rusty smiled as he handed Mr. Kimbel the old green board. "Yep, I agree. First, I want you to take a gander at this. It sure looks like a piece of one of them old Wells Fargo strongboxes," said Rusty, as he took a seat.

Mr. Kimbel studied it for a moment. "It certainly is. A real old timer at that. Where'd you get it?"

Rusty told Mr. Kimbel the whole story about how he had found the big iron box full of gold and that the board had been at the very bottom. He asked Mr. Kimbel if he had any idea how the iron box full of gold might have gotten there. Did he think that any of it belonged to Wells Fargo?

Mr. Kimbel considered the question for a moment. "As far as I know, all of the historical records of our great stagecoach days were completely destroyed by the San Francisco earthquake and fire in 1906. We would have no way of knowing or proving that all or, in fact, any of that gold once belonged to Wells Fargo."

"Did your outfit ever have any old iron boxes big as the one I described?" asked Rusty.

Mr. Kimbel tapped his fingers on the table thoughtfully. "Not that I know of. Your guess is as good as mine, but here's what I think." He told his story in the slow manner of a detective trying to unravel a mystery. "Three or four outlaws on horseback must have used a mule-drawn wagon to carry that iron box to the place where you found it. My guess is that it probably wasn't even half full at first, and then they made several more trips with stolen gold until they finally filled it. I'll bet that box of gold has been sittin' there since the 1860s, maybe even the 1850s. The gold could have been taken from miners working their claims, from assay offices, from banks, or from stagecoach shipments."

Amazed at all of these possibilities, Rusty asked, "What do you think happened to the robbers, that they didn't come back for it?"

Mr. Kimbel continued his slow but thoughtful analysis. "Well, Tom Bell was a real terror when it came to robbing miners panning gold in Central California. The law finally hung him about 1856. Rattlesnake Dick, who robbed a mule train of $80,000 in gold dust near Mt. Shasta, was shot in 1859. Nobody ever recovered any of that gold. There probably isn't a robber or miner alive today who ever touched your gold. Another possibility is train robberies. A number of our express cars were held up in the 1880s and '90s."

Eager to hear more, Rusty asked, "'bout how much gold did your Wells Fargo boxes hold?"

"Of course, those boxes weren't always shipped full, but I think about $21,000 in bagged gold dust is the most I ever heard of," answered Mr. Kimbel.

Anxious to conclude his business, Rusty said, "Well now, I wanna settle up. I'd like you to ship all my gold to the Frisco Mint. I want you to give $21,000 worth to Wells Fargo, along with this old board I just gave you."

"But Mr. Dalton, as I told you, with no old records, we have no legal claim to any of your gold."

Rusty stuck his hands in his pockets. "Well, Mr. Kimbel, it's like this. I'm not askin' you to claim it for Wells Fargo. It's just yours 'cuz I wanna give it back. Now, I got another thing to settle up. I guess you know, like everybody else, the sheriff owns two saloons and the biggest gamblin' joint in town. If some poor miner drinks a little too much in one of his saloons and then loses some money in his gamblin' joint, you know that the sheriff ain't goin' 'round givin' that poor feller his money back!"

Mr. Kimbel laughed as Rusty continued. "Yesterday, right in front of the whole town, the sheriff got to gamblin' with me. He lost, and I won. So if he comes crying 'round here wantin' to get his $20,000 back, tell 'im that Rusty already spent that $20,000, an' it's gone." Mr. Kimbel listened to Rusty with great interest. "I want you to put that $20,000 in your account books for Lo Fat, the cook at the Southern Hotel."

Mr. Kimbel looked directly at Rusty. "Are you certain you want to start spending your money like this?"

Rusty replied, "Well, I ain't gonna drink it all up or go to Frisco an' throw it 'round. I'm an old desert rat that's gonna stay in the desert! All my years I never done nothin' too bad or too good. I did do a couple of dumb things, like quittin' school, and never havin' no family or young'uns."

Impressed with Rusty's view of life, Mr. Kimbel listened carefully as he continued.

"Now, after all these years, I gotta chance to do somethin' smart. I wanna see Lo Fat go back to Frisco, be with his folks, and send Lee to a proper school. This is one chance I ain't gonna miss while I'm settlin' up!"

Mr. Kimbel shook his head in admiration. Here was a remarkable man if he'd ever seen one. Rusty signed the necessary papers to make the arrangements official.

As they walked toward the door, Mr. Kimbel commented, "You sure have a way of surprising everybody, including me. About ten days ago, while you were out of town, we had a total eclipse of the moon and an earthquake, both at the same time! Some folks around here are still arguing about who caused it, you or Charley Catch'um."

Rusty chuckled. "Well, I guess them fellers in the saloons gotta have somethin' to argue 'bout. Some of 'em probably see a total eclipse every weekend!"

Rusty walked down to the corral, where Joe Wilson greeted him as a celebrity. "Well, if it ain't the fastest gun in the West!"

Rusty grinned and asked, "How's the leader of my gang doin'? Did he get his oats?"

"Oh, that Zeke! I been spoilin' him real good." Then Joe became serious. "There was a feller here this mornin' to look at Zeke. Says he'd like to buy him for the circus."

Rusty was a little miffed. "Well, that feller's crazy, and anyway, his name ain't just Zeke, it's Zeke Dalton — the richest donkey in Nevada — maybe in the whole world! He don't need no job with that Barnum and Bailey outfit."

Changing the subject, Joe asked, "Figgerin' on getting yourself a spread, raisin' some cattle, and settlin' down?"

Rusty looked at the ground and nudged a rock with his boot.

"Naw, not me. The cattlemen call this place "10–30" country. A steer's gotta have a mouth ten feet wide and run thirty miles an hour to get anything to eat around here. None of that for me!"

Joe glanced over Rusty's shoulder. "Well, just look who's ridin' up here on that beautiful pinto of his!"

Rusty turned around and chuckled. "Sure looks like he's tracked me down this time."

Charley Catch'um dismounted slowly and walked ceremoniously over to Rusty and Joe. He wasn't smiling, but he wasn't wearing his usual grim expression. Charley held his head high and proudly raised his right hand in greeting. In his hand he held a beautiful eagle feather.

Rusty tipped his hat back a little as a friendly signal of recognition.

Charley directed his gaze at Rusty. In a deep, clear voice he said, "Brave man." He paused. "Wise man." Then he handed the big eagle feather to Rusty. Charley pointed at the eagle feather he wore in his own hat. With a little help from Joe, Rusty placed the feather in his own hat band and adjusted the angle.

Rusty was noticeably moved by this gesture from a man he had come to respect. His eyes smiled warmly as he said, "Charley, I want ya to know that I got no hard feelin's 'bout your trackin' me." He reached up and lightly touched the feather. "I ain't one of your people, but I'm mighty proud to have you for a friend."

Charley Catch'um did not smile, but people claimed that they had never seen him smile. Charley then turned to his beautiful pinto horse, with its two smaller eagle feathers tied to the mane and two more tied to leather thongs hanging from its ear. All four feathers dangled loosely beside the pinto's head. Charley removed the two feathers from his horse's ear, stepped over to

Zeke, who was tied to the gate post, and put the loop over Zeke's left ear. The two feathers hung just like the ones on the pinto. Charley patted Zeke on the neck and said, "Same, like horse."

Rusty was flabbergasted but finally regained his wits and said, "Charley, my people have an old sayin' when they get a real big surprise like this. They say 'You could of knocked me over with a feather!' Well, you durn well just did! Zeke and me won't ever forget this."

Charley Catch'um had a proud, serious look on his face as he mounted his horse. He didn't say good-bye, but as he turned to leave, Charley paused and looked at Rusty. He held up one hand, and Rusty did the same. Glancing at Zeke, a big, broad smile spread across Charley's face. Then he turned and rode off toward his village.

Joe turned to Rusty and said, "Indians sure ain't much for makin' long-winded speeches, but I'll bet his kids and grand-kids will hear a lot of long-winded stories 'bout you and Zeke."

Rusty grinned as he took the eagle feather out of his hat band and showed it to Joe. "You see these two bands of beads sewed on the quill right below the feather part here? Well, that's a Paiute sign." Rusty stroked the feather. "Them Indians have their own way of sayin' things. The red band of beads is for Charley. The white band is for me."

Joe reached out and touched the beads. "What does that mean?"

"Well, you see, while Zeke and me keep pokin' around in this desert country, we might run on to a band of Paiutes. If we do, we'll be with real friends. They'll know that I didn't shoot no eagle to get this feather," explained Rusty. Smiling with satis-faction, he put the feather back in his hat band, pointed to it and said, "Y'see, givin' a feller like me one of their feathers has a strong meanin' to them Paiutes. It's sorta like Charley and me was brothers. I'm gonna wear this everywhere I go."

Rusty patted Zeke on the neck. He asked Joe if he would get Zeke packed and ready and then bring him to the Southern Hotel an hour or so after sundown.

CHAPTER SEVENTEEN

The Richest Feller in Nevada

WHEN RUSTY ENTERED the Southern Hotel that evening, Mr. Nelson greeted him personally and then escorted him to a specially prepared table in the dining room next to the front window. A few people had gathered outside because they had heard that Rhyolite's new hero would be dining in the hotel that night. Rusty was having some trouble adjusting to the big difference a little gold dust made.

Lee came into the dining room with a big grin on his face. He told Rusty and Mr. Nelson that Lo Fat would be in as soon as he removed his apron. Lo Fat entered with the dignity befitting a royal guest. He was proud of his friend Rusty and equally proud of the fine dinner he had prepared. Without thinking, Rusty started to extend his hand to Lo Fat. Then, with a quick but awkward move, he used that hand to pull up his pants. Lo Fat smiled knowingly. He and Lee nodded slightly, each with hands together in the customary Chinese greeting.

Rusty said, "Well, Lo Fat, tonight Lee and I ain't peelin' potatoes out in back and you ain't 'busy-busy'!" They all laughed, remembering their first meeting.

Lo Fat responded, "No peel potato. No more. Rusty go Frisco with his frens. Okay?"

Rusty shook his head. "No Frisco! I'm a desert rat, and I'm gonna stay in this ol' desert."

Lo Fat looked puzzled. "Dessat rat?" He turned to Lee, who explained in Chinese. Then Lee said to Rusty, "My fatha neva hear 'dessat rat.' I tell him, jus' fun name people say."

Lo Fat, wanting to hold up his part of the conversation, said, "Rusty, dessat rat. Lo Fat, no dessat rat?"

Rusty thought for a moment, looked at Lee and smiled back. "A desert rat likes the ol' desert and lives in that ol' desert. Lo Fat, you certainly ain't no desert rat." Then, slowly, he said, "Lo Fat, you are a house mouse."

Lee immediately started laughing and, with a few more Chinese words, had Lo Fat laughing, too. When the waiter arrived with some egg flower soup, Rusty explored it carefully with his spoon and said, "You know this soup's pretty thin, but it's durn good." Lo Fat looked pleased.

Wanting to make his position clear when he presented Lo Fat with a Wells Fargo account book later in the evening, Rusty changed the subject. "You know, rich folks ain't all the same kind of critters. If one of them rich fellers from Frisco come over here to find gold with me, he wouldn't like it. Having to sleep all night on the durn ground, get up before daylight, splash cold water on his face, make a fire, and have a old tin of black coffee while bacon's frying wouldn't suit him. He probably wouldn't even like the smell of the sagebrush or the quiet ol' desert out there! No sirree! He just wouldn't like it."

Lo Fat understood this kind of talk without any interpretation by Lee. They listened closely as Rusty went on. "Now if I was to go to Frisco, them big hotels wouldn't have no place for

Zeke. Them fancy eating places don't even have no post out front where I could tie Zeke while I grabbed a bite of their grub! Funny thing is, I wouldn't fit in Frisco no better'n Zeke. So, we just don't belong there, an' we ain't *goin'* there."

Lee said a few words in Chinese to make sure his father fully understood what Rusty had said.

Rusty would never leave Zeke to go anywhere, including San Francisco. For the first time in his life, Rusty had a faithful friend in Zeke, and they depended on each other. The special bond between Rusty and Zeke was worth more than anything his gold could buy.

Their conversation was interrupted when the waiter served a tasty chicken and almond dish. Lo Fat and Lee ate with silverware instead of chopsticks. Things got kind of messy because Rusty was used to eating off his knee beside a campfire in the desert, so this dinner was an elegant occasion for him.

Rusty leaned back in his chair and said, "I guess you know that I got a lotta gold. It won't take much for me and Zeke to keep on pokin' 'round in the desert. So . . ." Rusty paused and reached into the pocket of his new shirt and took out a small Wells Fargo bankbook. Then he continued. "Lo Fat, you and Lee don't belong out here. You belong in Frisco with your wife and little girl. You oughtta start yourself a China food eating place and send Lee to school. Lee's a smart young feller, too durn smart to be a desert rat. So . . ." Rusty paused again out of fear that Lo Fat might refuse or not understand his gift.

He looked at Lee and then leaned close to Lo Fat. Almost in a whisper he said, "Lo Fat, you and me will both be proud of Lee someday, if he can only get *some* kinda chance. Now, I don't wanna lose my one chance right here and now of bein' proud of *somethin'*, so you just *gotta* take this here gift from Zeke and me." Rusty swallowed hard as he pressed the little book into Lo Fat's hand. Carefully, Lo Fat opened the little book, read the numbers, and absorbed what it all meant.

Lo Fat was at a complete loss for words and handed the book to Lee. Equally dumbfounded, Lee finally said, "All this money, gift for my fatha? Rusty gift?"

Rusty nodded. "Lee, you shared your dinner with me when we were strangers. Lo Fat, you shared your lucky rice with me when we didn't hardly know each other. Now we're all friends, an' I aim to share my good luck with you."

Lee and Lo Fat had a long discussion in Chinese, and both ended up all smiles. No one could think of anything else to say. They just sat there and enjoyed being together.

After the waiter brought in the shrimp and pea pods with some rice, Lo Fat excused himself, disappeared into the kitchen for a moment and returned to the table. A few minutes later, the waiter brought a bottle of the hotel's most expensive wine to their table. He poured a glass for Rusty and one for Lo Fat. After they each took a sip, their expressions showed that this dry, red wine tasted like vinegar to them. Immediately after the meal, the waiter brought two big cigars. Lo Fat put the wrong end in his mouth, but Rusty corrected that before lighting both cigars. They each took a puff and promptly put them in the ashtrays. Lo Fat could see that his wine and cigars were not a big hit. But because this *was* a big occasion, he thought that some kind of celebration was in order, so he proposed a toast. "Rusty say, Rusty dessat rat. Rusty say, Lo Fat house mouse." Then he and Rusty raised their wine glasses as Lo Fat said, "Lo Fat say, now we bigwigs — okay!"

They all laughed heartily. Just then, Lee stood up beaming with pride as the waiter approached their table carrying three big, beautiful slices of watermelon. Lee took the plate with the biggest piece and placed it in front of Rusty, while the waiter served the other two pieces.

Before Lee had a chance to say anything, Rusty exclaimed, "Well, if that don't beat all! Watermelon from Lee's own garden!"

"Fourth of July, Lee give one to Joe Wilson. Mr. Nelson buy all rest, for hotel," said Lo Fat proudly.

After one bite, Rusty closed his eyes to savor the taste. "This sure brings back old times. We always had watermelon on the Fourth of July. Us kids used to sit on the front porch to eat it so's we could have seed spittin' contests."

Lo Fat and Lee looked confused. They had never heard of such a contest. Rusty held one finger up to the side of his mouth to attract their attention. Then, barely moving his lips, sent a watermelon seed spurting out to land on the center of the table. Lo Fat exclaimed, "'merican people, funny people!"

Rusty shook his head in disbelief as he finished his piece of melon. "I never ate no watermelon this good in all my born days!"

Lo Fat and Lee got into an excited conversation in Chinese. Finally, Lee turned to Rusty. "My fatha cannot talk. He say words no good. He say 'thank you — good man' words too small. So my fatha happy and sad — same time."

Rusty beamed with pleasure. "Just tell him I'm as happy as he is. Tell him to remember that bag of lucky rice. If I was to say 'thank you' for that, my words would be too durn small just like his."

They finally finished their dinner and rose from the table. Rusty had already paid the manager for his room and the dinner, and Lo Fat paid for the wine and cigars. Rusty walked slowly to the front entrance of the hotel, where he could see Joe

Wilson and Zeke waiting for him. Lo Fat and Lee came out on the front walk to say good-bye. They all looked at each other, not knowing how to part. Suddenly, Lo Fat extended his hand to Rusty in an American-style handshake. Rusty looked Lo Fat in the eye and, with a firm grip, silently shook his hand. Rusty was pleased beyond words. Then Lee did the same, and they both had a long, warm good-bye handshake. No one smiled.

A crowd of people had gathered for another glimpse of their new hero. Someone yelled, "Ain't you gonna buy everybody in town a drink like ol' Death Valley Scotty always does?"

Rusty stood on the hotel boardwalk and looked out at the whole crowd. "Can *anyone* in this town ever remember buyin' *me* a drink?"

A murmur went through the crowd as people looked at each other. An uncomfortable silence fell over them. As no one said a word, Rusty resumed, "If any feller here can remember when or where he bought me a drink, I'll buy him a whole barrel of whiskey."

Rusty waited. Only the chirping of crickets broke the silence. No one spoke up, and no one stepped forward. Rusty questioned them again. "You mean *nobody* in this whole town can ever remember buyin' me a drink?" After a slight pause, he said, "Well, I guess maybe that shows you what drinkin' does to your memory!"

Rusty's joke eased the tension in the crowd, and everyone started laughing. Then, with a big smile, Rusty said, "Only one feller in this town did buy me a drink! He's standin' right there." Rusty pointed to Lo Fat, who was still standing on the board-walk with Lee. Lo Fat smiled after Lee explained to him what Rusty had said.

Rusty stepped into the street, untied Zeke, and offered a

Chinese good-bye gesture to Lo Fat and Lee. As he turned to go, someone in the crowd said, "Joe here was telling us all about your feather. You gonna be a chief?"

Everyone laughed. Rusty grinned and touched the feather. "Well, you can laugh if you want, but I gotta tell you that this feather means somethin' special, somethin' that all your money and all my gold can't buy."

As Rusty was smoothing the feather between his fingers, someone else said, "You always bragged you'd be the richest feller in Nevada some day. You sure *will* be if you never buy anything with all that gold."

Rusty thought for a minute. Then, with that old twinkle in his eyes, he quietly remarked, "Well, I been thinkin' a lot 'bout that, and I'm beginnin' to wonder if maybe I *ain't* the richest feller in Nevada, with or without the durn gold."

The people were puzzled by Rusty's comment. Some of them began to realize that this strange, old fellow, at whom everyone had poked fun, was actually quite a remarkable man. The crowd watched silently as Rusty and Zeke ambled slowly down Golden Street, headed for the ol' desert that Rusty loved.

As they neared the top of the ridge west of town, Rusty paused to look back at the lights of Rhyolite. With a wistful look in his eyes, he patted Zeke on the neck and said, "Well, little feller, just look at them lights down there, twinklin' like they was diamonds in the desert." Rusty shook his head back and forth slowly as he continued, "It's real pretty from here, but that town ain't for us no more. Time was when me and you could fiddle 'round down there and the folks paid us no mind. Now, I wouldn't get no peace tryin' to live 'round here." He went on talking as he unloaded a small sack of oats, even though Zeke just stood there blinking his eyes. "Folks would want me to buy 'em drinks, loan 'em money, and they'd be fussin' and stewin' about something all the time." Zeke started to pay more attention when he noticed Rusty opening the bag of oats. Rusty continued, "Maybe we oughtta head on over to see ol' Death Valley Scotty one of these days. He's got this whole durn thing figured out. He just comes to town when he wants to raise a ruckus and then gits!" Rusty opened the bag of oats and Zeke poked his head into it for a few nibbles. He smiled as he noticed his little partner's quick response and continued, "You know, just bein' a durn little ol' donkey ain't all that bad!"

Rusty and Zeke turned their backs on the city lights, and as they continued over the ridge, Rusty said, "There's a little draw over yonder — just a couple of miles or so. Maybe we oughtta camp down there for a spell till we get our thinkin' caps on straight again." They found a place that had a good view of the freight yards about four miles away.

The following morning Rusty and Zeke crossed the ridge on their way back to town. Rusty paused to take in the expansive view of Rhyolite and said, "Yep, this will be our last good-bye to Lee and his pa. This durn town won't never be the same again."

CHAPTER EIGHTEEN

Mr. Dalton Was Right, All Right

THE DAY BEFORE Lo Fat and Lee were scheduled to leave for San Francisco, Lee went down to Joe Wilson's corral to see Jamie. Before Lee could say anything, she started telling him that her father had arranged to go to the hotel the next morning to pick up Lo Fat's baggage and take it to the railroad station. Jamie was busily grooming Beans because he had been chosen to carry the small load of luggage to the station. Lee patted Beans on the neck, pleased that Joe and Jamie had thought of his father.

Changing the subject, Lee told Jamie that he wanted her to have his watermelon patch. If she watered it every other day, five or six big melons would ripen in a week or so.

Jamie was pleased and promised to take good care of his wonderful melons. Then, she stepped a little closer to Lee and said softly, "I'll be at the station tomorrow to say good-bye." She didn't want her father to hear, because he knew that she should be in school at that time.

Lee actually blushed; then he started walking somewhat self-consciously up the street. When he turned around to take one final peek at Jamie, he waved goodbye. She giggled and waved back. Among all of the kids in Rhyolite, Jamie was Lee's only friend and she was a good friend at that.

Lo Fat and Lee arrived at the station an hour early the next morning. The train was scheduled to leave at 11 o'clock. Joe took Beans back to the corral after unloading the luggage. To all appearances, it was just a quiet, humdrum day in Rhyolite.

About 10 o'clock, Jamie stood up in her classroom at school. Taking a deep breath, she steadied herself with one hand on the edge of her desk. "Miss Holbrook, I have a special announcement to make."

Curiously, Miss Holbrook said, "Yes, Jamie, what is it?"

Jamie looked at the class. "Well, a good friend of mine is leaving on the train today in about an hour. My friend's name is Lee." Jamie looked down at the floor for a second and then back up at Miss Holbrook. "He rescued my pony, Beans, from some horse thieves. He also gave me his watermelon patch." She lifted her head and looked around the room at her classmates. "Most of you know about him, but none of you have ever tried to get to know him or to understand him. My father told me that Rusty Dalton gave Lee's father some gold so they could leave here and go back to San Francisco. Lee can go to a good school there."

Jamie paused to catch her breath as she continued, "Remember all those firecrackers we heard on the Fourth of July? — Well, they belonged to Lee. He wanted to share them with all of us. He did it the only way he knew how." Feeling her anger mount, Jamie spoke a little louder and faster. "Lee really believes that this is *his* country, just like it's your country and my country, but he isn't even allowed to attend school. I'm ashamed of Rhyolite, and I'm ashamed of this school!" She turned to the teacher in defiance. "Miss Holbrook, I'm not asking for your permission. I don't care if you make me scrub the blackboard and clap the erasers for the rest of the year. I'm leaving school right now to say good-bye to my friend, Lee." Jamie slammed a book shut and marched out of the room.

Miss Holbrook was stunned, and the classroom buzzed with the students' whispered remarks. Miss Holbrook knew this was it. She had to do something. Tapping her desk with a ruler she said, "Now, class, I have something to say, and I want all of you to listen carefully." Everyone stopped whispering and listened to her.

"All of you know that Jamie has always been a leader and one of the best students in our school. It took a lot of courage to do what Jamie just did!" She cleared her throat and looked out of the window as she thought of what to say next.

"I had a long talk with Mr. Dalton over a month ago. When he first came in here, I didn't know what to think about him. But after I got to know and understand him, I have to tell you that he is one of the finest men I have ever met." She continued, "Mr. Dalton wanted me to explain why Lee couldn't attend our school, and I did not have a good answer. I guess I *still* don't have a good answer. But I want all of you to hear one of the things he said to me that morning: 'People just understanding people is all it takes. Your kids won't get this understanding out of their schoolbooks.'"

She paused and continued, "So you see, what I thought of Mr. Dalton before I knew and understood him and what you probably thought of Lee without knowing or understanding him are exactly the same. We've all of us been wrong!"

Miss Holbrook looked around the room and asked, "Can any one of you tell me in your own words what Mr. Dalton *meant* about understanding?"

A boy in the back of the room finally raised his hand. The student said, "Mr. Dalton said that maybe we ought to understand some stuff that ain't in our books!" A number of kids laughed, but no one else volunteered.

A feeling of despair came over Miss Holbrook as she realized that Mr. Dalton was right. Understanding people comes from something more than books or just talking about it in the classroom. Now that Lee and his father were leaving town, it seemed too late to do anything.

Suddenly inspired, Miss Holbrook announced to the class, "We have one last chance to learn what Mr. Dalton was talking about."

She selected a couple of schoolbooks, put them under her arm, and blew the drill whistle that hung around her neck. "James, you are in charge of the first section; Mary, the second section; Amy, the third section; and Charles, you handle the rear guard. We are going out in front of the school right now and line up like we did for the Fourth of July parade. Each section leader will call out the cadence loudly: One, two, three, four! One, two, three, four!" The kids scrambled outside. What fun! A parade during school hours!

After they were properly assembled, Miss Holbrook said, "We are going to march, not straggle, right up Golden Street to the railroad station. Then we can split up and do our best to say goodbye to Lee and his father."

The procession moved out of the schoolyard and up Golden Street. People came running from all directions and asked what the parade was about. Miss Holbrook simply responded, "We're marching for good citizenship."

It was surprising how many people came to watch. They tagged along beside the kids and asked questions, just as Miss

Holbrook had hoped they would. The kids who were to attend the afternoon class at school came running from their homes and the playground to join the parade. A bunch of the fellows hanging around the saloons came out, waved their hats, and hooted and hollered. They had no idea what was going on, but to them fun was fun, and many joined the growing crowd. Sheriff Tucker came up the street half-running and half-walking to see what was happening.

As they approached the station, Miss Holbrook hurried ahead of the children, hoping that she could find Lo Fat and Lee before the train pulled out.

Her search ended when she heard Jamie's excited voice from the rear car of the train. Jamie had been there long enough to help Lee and his father find their seats. Then she had persuaded them to join Rusty on the rear observation platform of the car for their last view of Rhyolite. The rear car platform was the same one the presidential candidates used to make political speeches when the train stopped in small towns.

Miss Holbrook was overjoyed; what a perfect setting for their farewell to Lo Fat and Lee! Jamie quickly scrambled down the steps from the last car to meet her teacher. Miss Holbrook put her arms around Jamie and laughed as she proudly said to her, "The kids and I want to help you clap erasers for the rest of the year!"

Still standing on the observation platform with Rusty, Lo Fat and Lee were completely amazed at what was going on. When Rusty heard a sudden burst of steam from the engine, he said his goodbyes and hurried off the train. Lo Fat and Lee smiled as they watched Rusty join Joe Wilson, who was holding on to Zeke at the edge of the crowd.

Miss Holbrook quickly worked her way through the crowd

that had gathered around the rear of the train. Mr. Nelson had just reached up and handed Lo Fat a small basket of oranges for their trip. He made room for Miss Holbrook, who held the books up as high as she could. Lee leaned way over to take them. The crowd was so noisy that Miss Holbrook had to raise her voice when she said, "These books are a farewell gift from the whole school."

Lee looked at the books, then took and held them close to his chest. He looked out at all of the kids and then back at Miss Holbrook, who said, "Lee, I'm . . . I'm sorry. I'm so sorry."

Lee smiled at Miss Holbrook and then glanced at Jamie, who was standing next to her. Jamie beamed as she waved to him. Lee had never seen anyone look so excited and so happy. Rusty was right. Jamie was a real friend, not just a watermelon friend. Lee was quick to smile because his eyes were growing watery.

As the train began to roll slowly out of the station, Lee and his father looked back at Rusty and Zeke again. Rusty waved his hat at them to keep their attention. Then he surprised them. Quickly putting his hat back on his head, Rusty made a loose fist with his right hand and held it in his cupped left hand. He bowed slightly and moved his hands up and down in true Chinese style. Lo Fat and Lee were delighted with Rusty's thoughtful gesture. Lee turned to see his father's reaction. Lo Fat had clasped his hands together and was returning this sign of respect. He lifted his head after a slight bow and smiled, his eyes shut. But Lee could see a tear roll down one of his father's cheeks. The kids yelled and shouted as the train cars jolted and a big puff of steam went up in the air. Lee realized that he probably would never see Rhyolite or any of these people again. As the train rolled farther out of the station, a number of the boys ran after it, waving and whistling. Lee knew that Rusty must have had something to do with this surprise farewell at the train station. He held one book in each hand, raised them up above his head, and waved them at the crowd. A big cheer went up. Everyone stood and watched as the train went around a curve and the whistle blew, "Wooooooo — woo-woo!"

Joe Wilson put his arm around Jamie's shoulder. Big tears rolled down her cheeks.

"Now, now," said Joe, "what's the matter here?"

Trembling, Jamie said, "Dad, I can't help it. I feel so good inside. I just can't help crying!"

As Miss Holbrook turned to regroup the students into their parade formation, she noticed some angry stares from spectators. A few men shook their heads and gave her some downright dirty looks. She recalled Mr. Dalton's "reminder" that many grownups are fairly set in their ways. She realized right then that the real problem was not leaving Rhyolite with Lee and his father.

Miss Holbrook was not a quitter. She held her head high and blew her whistle. She was surprised at how quickly the children responded and lined up properly for the march back to school. As the parade got underway, two women approached her. One of them said, "We just want you to know that we're proud that our town has a person like you." She looked at the women for a moment and said quietly, "I thank you for that, Mrs. Roberts." Then she turned to give a short blast on her whistle.

As the children marched down Golden Street, they passed a saloon. A drunk swayed through the swinging doors and stepped out into the street. He took off his hat and, as he waved it, he yelled, "Hey, teach — your kids done good!"

With that, he staggered back into the saloon. Miss Holbrook smiled with the knowledge that she, at least, had Rusty, two women, and one drunk on her side. But, what about the children? Was she really steering them in the right direction, or were they all just out for a lark, a break from school?

As Miss Holbrook marched along with her class, Jamie began humming the only song all of the children knew. Spontaneously, the students joined her as they all began singing the familiar lyrics of the patriotic song that they sang every morning before school. All of the people on the streets were familiar with the words, as well. "My country, 'tis of thee, sweet land of liberty, of thee we sing. Long may our land be bright, with freedom's holy light. . . ."

The children sang verse after verse. Miss Holbrook stopped and fell behind the marching children as she thought about what they were doing. She realized that in the past the children had sung the song and the words, but they hadn't fully appreciated or understood the meaning of those words. Suddenly, she felt proud: her students, her children, were singing without her, were singing from their hearts! At last, the words "my country," "liberty," and "freedom" meant something real to them, because now these words included people, people they really *knew*, people like Lee, and Lo Fat. Miss Holbrook's lips began to quiver, but she held back the tears. Holding her head high, she quickened her pace to rejoin the parade.

Rusty and Zeke were plodding along on the dusty road south of town. When the students' voices became so loud that he could hear them singing, Rusty stopped and turned around. He removed his hat and waved it as high as he could. When he caught Miss Holbrook's attention, she smiled broadly and waved her arm back and forth.

As she marched along, Miss Holbrook thought to herself,

"People, just understanding people, and facing up to what you believe in . . . Mr. Dalton was right, all right."

Miss Holbrook turned to wave once more, but Rusty and Zeke had already disappeared into the desert. But the little smile on her face slowly became a large smile as she heard a faint sound from way in the distance. "Hee-haw! Hee-haw!"

Colophon

A Bag of Lucky Rice has been set in Minion, a typeface designed for Adobe Systems by Robert Slimbach in 1990. An offshoot of the designer's researches during the development of Adobe Garamond, Minion's development hybridized the characteristics of numerous Renaissance sources into a single calligraphic hand. Unlike many faces developed exclusively for digital typesetting, drawings for Minion were transferred to the computer early in the design phase, preserving much of the freshness of the original concept. Conceived with an eye toward overall harmony, its capitals, lower-case, and numerals were carefully balanced to maintain a well-groomed "family" resemblance both between roman and italic and across the full range of weights. A decidedly contemporary face, anchored to no single historical model, Minion makes free use of the qualities the designer found most appealing in the types of the fifteenth and sixteenth centuries. Crisp drawing and a narrow set width make Minion an economical and easy-going book type, and even its name reinforces its adaptable, affable, and almost self-effacing nature, referring as it does to a small size of type, a faithful or favored servant, and a kind of peach.

❧ ❧ ❧

Design and composition by
Carl W. Scarbrough